# BE MY DESTINY:

## VOWS FROM THE BEYOND

### BOOK THREE OF THE *KASTEEL VREDERIC* SERIES

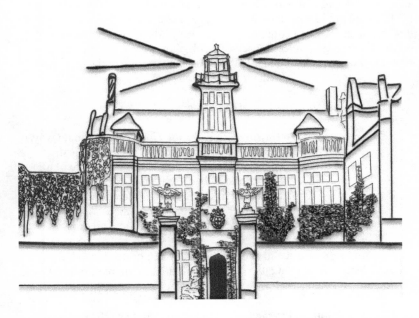

*"Within sacred vows of the dreamland, we belong to one another, yet I keep my lantern of hope glowing. Physically may I be your destination and you be my destiny."*

## Ann Marie Ruby

Published in the United States of America, 2021.

ISBN-10: 0-578-91488-3

ISBN-13: 978-0-578-91488-6

# DEDICATION

*"The world becomes one home through the blessed travels of the travelers. For the travelers gather within their chest, memories from across the globe and paint a portrait, they call one world, one home."*

I have dedicated this book to three incredible countries on this Earth. A traveler I had become as my footsteps had landed upon these sacred places. Forever as I traveled, I left my love for them and brought back their eternally blessed love with me. This pledge of love has tied us into a union throughout time. For this reason, I dedicate my book *Be My Destiny: Vows From The Beyond* to these blessed countries as follows.

## India:
## Land Of Mystery

A majestic land, where the sun rises and sets as the land evolves all her inhabitants within a magical relationship from the beyond. Reincarnation is a sacred belief kept sacredly within the hearts of a lot of people within this land. This belief has crossed time and tide as she has landed all over this globe. This belief was encircled within a religious group yet now is a fact even science cannot disapprove, as witnessed by humans across the globe.

This mystical sacred belief gave me the inspiration to look into the journey of reincarnation as I believed in this journey first and had published my other non-fictional books. Now for the first time, within this fictional book, I have brought my characters to life through this enchanted theory I too believe in. My life journey has taught me this is not just a theory, but a fact.

I admire the people of India as this land has gifted the world evidence of reincarnation. I had personally visited this land and was inspired by her geographical beauty as well as the amazing hospitality of her citizens. From the small roadside tea stalls, to the rickshaw drivers and the tour guides, this country has taken my heart as I shall forever love her throughout time.

Thank you, India, for giving me this amazing experience. For this reason, I have taken my fictional characters through this mystical country. Throughout time, I shall be a friend of this nation as she has gifted me with amazing, graceful hospitality.

# The United States Of America: Land Of The Free

My home, my blessed land, is where all her citizens and guests find graceful love and welcome. My life is entwined within this land as she gave me all that life can expect from a mother. This land of the free is where so many dreams are made and lived within every day. Where else can you dream the dream, and live it in peace and harmony? Within this land, we are allowed to believe in reincarnation or any other beliefs without being discriminated against.

I have been lucky to live here as I brought my characters to life within this beautiful land. Washington State is my home state, where the mountains touch the sky. Within the foothills, we find amazing green valleys and lakes, creating a picturesque portrait to satisfy my imaginative mind and my imaginary canvas.

Nevertheless, all of this is alive within the eyes of this human as this is my home, where I live. My characters also made their home here. Thank you for being my home, as you have inspired this land to be the home state for my characters.

The Netherlands:
Land Of My Dreams

I think of windmills, flowers, the smell of fresh baked stroopwafels, Gothic castles, romantic canoe rides, and colorful romantic cottages where dreams do come true, when I think of the Netherlands. The most loving and ever understanding very truthful voices of the Dutch inhabitants have restored my faith in humanity. The Dutch citizens have proved to me my own quote, "work for each other, not against" as they have united all race, color, and religion, and for proof of this, the Peace Palace stands tall for all to visit her.

Within this land, His Majesty King Willem-Alexander, Her Majesty Queen Máxima, and the honorable Prime Minister Mark Rutte ride their bikes amongst the citizens. They do this to be with one another as they all work for one another not against. All are equally blessed as they call this beautiful country, the Netherlands.

I had traveled to this land, after I wrote my book *Spiritual Lighthouse: The Dream Diaries Of Ann Marie Ruby*. I have also written my book *The Netherlands: Land Of My Dreams*, then I wrote my book *Everblooming: Through The Twelve Provinces Of The Netherlands,* and the historical romance fiction *Kasteel Vrederic* series, all based in this country.

After all of these books, now I bring to you yet another fictional romance. These amazing journeys through this magical land, and my blessed dreams, led me to do research and write this romance novel. I have always said my favorite vacation destination is the Netherlands. Now through the tunnel of time, I have weaved my characters to life within this blessed land known to all as the Netherlands.

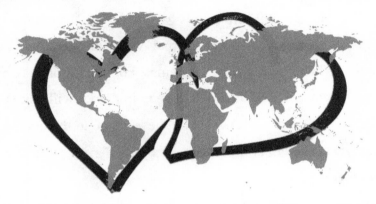

India, the United States of America, and the Netherlands have made a huge impact for which I have personally developed as a peace-loving citizen of this world. I have dedicated this book to these wonderful countries as just by visiting through the pages of my characters, I saw how unique and different, yet similar we all are. The bridge of union between all race, color, and religion is love.

The Lord's eternal blessings for all is love. No land or religion, or even belief can separate true love or the eternal lovers. I believe love is the bridge that unites all with their beloved even beyond life. For where there is love, all other obstacles can be eliminated if only you the beloved believe. For remember the only enemy true lovers have are themselves, for if they don't accept or acknowledge their feelings and accept one another to begin their ever after love story, no one else can.

No strength from this world or the beyond can separate true love for the eternal vows always shall be between the two beloved twin flames. For what is one life or seven as throughout time, I believe twin flames will unite in life or even in death. Destiny might take one to the other or not, yet throughout time and tide, they will be created for one another.

Believe in yourself and your true love for where there is belief, faith, and hope, there is always a way. You the world citizen, wherever on Earth you are, do awaken at the first sight of dawn and let your country, your hometown, know you love her. This Earth is beautiful as I have found these three countries on Earth give my characters their identity as blessed twin flames.

Love is the eternal truth that binds all of us into one home. I believe all twin flames from around the globe will awaken for one another crossing all the bridges of differences for they shall sing like the nightingales across the globe calling one another,

*Be My Destiny: Vows From The Beyond.*

# TABLE OF CONTENTS

# PART ONE:

# VOWS OF ANADHI NEWHOUSE

# PROLOGUE

*" 'Forever be mine' whispers of the night became my heartbeat as I infinitely shall keep my vows, through life or beyond death, forever I am yours."*

*Anadhi Newhouse writing her diary in her home in greater Seattle, Washington.*

P ouring rain falls into the Puget Sound and becomes a part of her. As the Puget Sound travels through Washington State, she kisses the ocean and changes her name to become a part of the Pacific Ocean and becomes immortal.

An epic love story is born through the rivers, the oceans, and the seas that somehow, in some way meet up and become immortal. I too want to unite with my twin flame and through our love, become immortal as we unite and become one. Come and enter my life as I am Anadhi Newhouse and this is my diary.

Life has taught me to keep my eternal vows given to my eternally beloved. It was easy as I love him beyond time and tide. No one alive or dead could take him away from me. I wondered what if he came in front of me, would I let him keep my vows or would I break my vows for him? For you, I live and for you, I shall live even beyond death, yet how do I find you for myself and only myself?

You are thinking that is a strange question as how could the love of my life, the person I had taken the vows for, or with, break my vows? For you see, I have met my twin flame in my dreams. Yes, it's just as true as meeting him in reality. We have taken our wedded vows and promised to be one another's throughout time, or until we meet in reality. I have seen him in different forms calling out to me. The door of dreams brought to me another door my mother believes in, called the door of reincarnation.

Every night as I had fallen asleep on my bed, I time traveled to another world, another land and time where I was within the embrace of my eternally beloved. Promises were made and kept yet as dawn reached my windows, I had awakened to a very lonely bed. I saw no sign of my twin flame, yet only the heartbeats of promises kept.

With the first sign of dawn, I was separated from him physically yet my mind, body, and soul I had left with him. I never asked myself if he remembers me or why I should keep the promises I had left in a dream. For I know, my heart has promised herself to her twin flame and this promise will stay with her through life and even beyond death. I knew I had to find him but how do I find him was the unanswered question of my life. I left the question at the door of faith.

The next question was how would we know each other? Would we accept one another's looks and forms as humans living on Earth, or would we not recognize one another even if we are left facing one another? In my dreams, I had told my beloved I would accept him and forever be only his. He promised he would find me and be only mine, yet I wondered how this miracle would become.

He spoke to me in a dream on a very star-filled, dark night as he held on to me, "Who said time is the only thing that keeps on moving? Time holds still as love crosses over time. Crossing over generation after generation, for the only truth that unites all and survives even eternity is but our love. Forever yours I was and shall always be."

I wondered but my beloved, my fear is what if for me, you don't even accept me? For I pray our vows don't become our boundary when we finally do meet.

His words were, "Be my destiny, these are my vows from the beyond."

Come and travel through the pages of my diary to see how I found him and even then I had to ask the hard and cruel destiny, but why do you keep on testing me? As my beloved had asked me to be his eternally, I had written my eternal vows, a song, a poem for only him.

## BE MY DESTINY: VOWS FROM THE BEYOND

"Destined to destiny, life is,"
Says fate.
Yet, I ask fate,
What about the destined traveler?
Where in life lies her will,
Her want,
Her need,
Her wishes?
If you, fate,
Have already predestined her end,
Then why is she the traveler
And not you?
For this traveler, this destined,

Shall always keep her vows,
For I shall never break the chains,
Linked to my twin flame.
Her given promises,
Not you nor life,
Not even my fate,
Could take away or break up,
My given vows to my other half.
Forever his I am destined to be,
In life or even beyond death.
Vows I have taken only with you,
Only for you.
For as we had recited
Throughout time,
*BE MY DESTINY:*
*VOWS FROM THE BEYOND.*

Yet, I had kept on asking my destiny to not betray me of my love. I realized I must keep my vows for they are my answered prayers to my own question. I kept on hoping he could hear the heartbeats, the heartbeats of his twin flame. Be my destiny my beloved for these are my vows from this life and the beyond.

# CHAPTER ONE:

## *Brain Fog, Dreams, Or Reality*

*"One either believes destiny is destined to follow from behind or believes in one's own dreams for they replace destiny through determination which guides you to your destination."*

*Anadhi Newhouse standing by the lagoon, deep in her own world of thoughts. Was she dreaming or were her dreams pulling her twin flame to her even in the daytime?*

The rain pouring outside was like a romantic dance rhythm. I could close my eyes and see beautiful couples, little children, or even strangers dancing within this mystical rhythm. The musical rhythm of nature flooded my soul as the rain was pouring and banging on the windows. The wind was dancing her part as she included the trees and all of nature to partake in this classical love story of nature. Sleep had left my eyes as we had said our goodbyes, not trying to help each other for we both knew it was not even worth trying.

I love the quiet nights when nothing can be heard, except the classical music of Mother Nature. All the memories from the memory lane kick back in as I feel lonely. I was lonely all my life. This thirst of loneliness, nothing could fulfill. My dreams from the lonely nights were my saving grace. Yet now my tired body wouldn't allow my blessed dreams to guide me.

The classical music outside just added a new member to their group as lightning started to strike for she knew it was her cue. After Mr. Thunder drums his part, lightning knows she is on next. I could hear my grandmother snoring through all of this adding to nature's musical concert outside.

I wanted to check on her as she is one of the only surviving relatives I have. It is so nice to watch her. I feel a warm comfort running through my soul. She is the most loving, giving, and happy person I know who exists on Earth. She battles all the sorrows on Earth with love, joy, and laughter while she brings smiles back on the faces she encounters.

I wondered if she was dreaming as her eyes were moving as if she was in the REM cycle. My life has brought me to this door where I have become an expert in dream studies. Scientists have proven dreams to be the truth of the beyond. Yet, what we see and why is a mystery. I live for my door of dreams to allow me in and find out all the proofs of the beyond. This household has interlinking dreams where we all see the same person calling upon us from the beyond.

The sounds of footsteps on the fallen leaves outside again struck me as I went to the living room of our ranch house, a beautiful cottage we call home. Our mystical cottage is blooming with all different roses, rhododendron, azaleas, climbing jasmine, clematis, wisterias growing over the bamboo arbors, apple trees and grape vines growing in the backyard, and a porch in the front with a swing for Grandmother and me.

The covered wraparound porch travels to the magnificently fenced backyard. There is a very old stone bridge crossing over the lagoon and the pouring rain makes all of this so surreal, a picture frame of the Creator. The stone bridge has a lot of historical events linked to her as this was built in the early eighteenth century.

My grandmother is a Christian and I am a Hindu-Christian. My name, Anadhi Newhouse, was given to me by my Indian mother and American father. Anadhi means "infinite" as this name was given to my mother in her dreams. This name is given to boys and girls, as this name also means Hindu Supreme God, Krishna, who does not have any end or beginning. I am a twenty-five-year-old Indian-American woman, five feet, four inches tall, with olive skin, brown eyes, and dark, long black hair.

Today, I live with my American grandmother of European descent, a very tall and slender woman with pale white skin, brown hair, and deep forest green eyes. We love one another and have made a haven in peace as life had put us in this picture of union by force. Mother Earth has her own stories as she is the only witness to our story and many others.

The sound of someone walking in the park kept on arising me in a different way like a pull, a magnet. I saw a strong light shining in the lagoon. It was cold. I picked up my white robe and slippers and I walked onto the porch to see if any of our friendly deer were on a nightly stroll and wanted my company.

There, I saw him standing in the rain watching over me. Even from so far, I could see his brown hair and his six-foot or maybe taller figure just standing in this pouring rain. I thought he was different as if the rain could not touch him. Even in the pouring rain, he was dry. In the dark night where nothing could be seen, I could see him as though he was glowing. It looked like light came from within him. He must have been an angel in disguise.

He was standing in the lagoon or I should say on the lagoon, as if that's how all travel. I was not afraid of him for I had seen him so many times, it was natural to me now. I know I wait for him all night and the nights I don't see him, I long for him even more wondering why he has not come in my dreams. Then, I see him like this.

I wondered is he dreaming about me, and traveling to me through his dreams? Does he not know I have been waiting for him, just to see him even just once, a small glimpse of him? I live for him, I want to run to him and not let go, but fear stops me in place.

I was not afraid of him, but feared what if my longing, my heartbeat, my need to hold him just once, takes him far away from me. I just wanted to see him for I knew in my dreams, I would get visits from him. I had waited for days to see him and after a period of three weeks, I finally got to see him. I had researched how I saw him and realized it's some sort of an awakening dream, where a person's soul travels to his or her beloved.

It's just like how a mother knows her children are in trouble or need help. I guess twin flames too can travel to one another through dreams, fog, or through the pull of love just to be there when there is a need. I wanted to ask, why have you not come in my dreams? What was wrong? You know I wait all night to see you. How is this fair? I get to see you from far away, but even that you take away from me. Do you share my feelings or are they just my own feelings?

I kept all my feelings in my heart as we never spoke, but just watched each other and knew these feelings of mine were answered by him just the way he too watched me. Teardrops fail me as they fall without warning and they don't stop. I felt a warm set of hands on my shoulder. As I jerked, I saw Grandmother holding me from the back.

I started to cry as I told her, "I had fallen asleep on the swing and saw him again. I really think he was here and somehow he can travel, maybe in his sleep. Or, through my pull of calls to him."

My grandmother's name, Miranda Newhouse, describes her perfectly as Miranda means worthy and admirable. William Shakespeare must have thought about my grandmother when he named his female character "Miranda" for his play. I compared my grandmother to this character as my grandmother always dressed elegantly, yet she was so nice and welcoming if you get to know her. Yet I know people would see her very differently as they judge the book by the cover not the inside.

I am biracial and sometimes feel lost. I feel like I am not typical anything as I am asked about my ethnicity so many times. I try to ignore the subject as it comes with a lot of memories. In India, everyone inquired about my ethnicity as I have so much of my father in me. In America, everyone asks about my ethnicity as I have so much of my mother in me. From a young age, I fought for myself and told all inquirers, I have through love combined two countries, two ethnicities, and two religions in one, that's me in person. I came back to today as I saw my grandmother watching me.

I asked my grandmother, "Did you see him?"

She answered, "Yes, crystal clear, as if he is made from light and his body glows in the dark. I feel like you two can speak mind to mind. You need to ask him what is going on. This is not right. I see you waiting for him, crying for him, and longing for him. It will drive you insane. I am worried for you. You need to go out and date. Have a normal life. What is going on? Does Hinduism say anything about this? I sure know we call these ghostly encounters. Dreams are normal but these interlinking dreams of him and how he appears to warn you or save you is not normal."

I told her, "I don't know if anyone on Earth knows what is going on, but I am not going to tell anyone, and you won't either for this is my life and I live it my way. Grandmother, I see him in my dreams and wonder if he too sees me in his dreams. Do you think he is asleep and dreaming? Does he dream travel through the tunnel of light?"

My grandmother said, "Sweetheart, sometimes the elders know more than you think, but the time must be right."

I told her, "Maybe it's the door of reincarnation. He must have been reincarnated, and his last life form comes to me or maybe this life form comes to me through the pull of love. I am guessing it's the powers of being twin flames."

I saw darkness faded as we were greeted by dawn. The kitchen smelled of fresh baked bread, omelets, and coffee. I walked in and knew Grandmother was busy making breakfast. She gave up meat when I walked into her life. I included eggs as she gave up so much more for me. We called our family, pescatarians.

I have no idea how long I was on the porch. My nights passed by me, without realizing that time passes by giving us no notice she is passing. I found myself on the porch swing sleeping with a warm blanket as I woke up most mornings waiting for him and falling asleep. I see him in my dreams as we have a life together in that realm. For a long time, I have lived this dual life.

Every day, I watch couples walking hand in hand as I only long to see him one more time. Every day, I wait for the arrival of my angel in disguise. Ever since the horrible accident that had changed my life and brought us together and introduced me to Erasmus.

My grandmother and I have been waiting for another miracle to take place. I watch out for anyone called Erasmus and hope he is going to be on my porch soon, sitting with me. With my luck, he will probably pull me to his porch.

Maybe my love, my twin flame Erasmus, will arrive like a miracle from the stars. Every night, he promises me he will try to break all barriers to unite with me as I too give him my vows, eternally yours I will try my best to break all the barriers. I asked my love to guide me or help me through this cloudy period of my life. For were these dreams, or was I living in a fog, or was all of this a part of my reality I live in?

Life was a miracle and at times, a nightmare as through a nightmare I had entered Seattle, Washington with my parents. Unfortunate and unforeseen events had changed my life forever. I wonder at times if everything that was happening to me were brain fog, dreams, or reality?

# CHAPTER TWO:

## *Destined To Seattle, Washington*

*"Fate escapes no one yet we must hold on to fate and tell her we will keep believing in you as you too must believe we will keep on rewriting you."*

*Anadhi Newhouse was destined to be in Seattle yet she did not know why and how her destiny would keep her alive.*

ashington State gives greetings to her neighbor country Canada at the northern border and the US state Oregon at the south. Washington State, known as the Evergreen State, is framed within sixty-four mountain ranges. She is an artist's dream portrait. This marvelous state is framed with snow-covered Olympic Mountains and the Cascade Range which Mount Rainier and Mount St. Helens are a part of. Mount Rainier and Mount St. Helens are two of the most dangerous volcanoes in the US.

The peaceful Puget Sound which eventually runs into the Pacific Ocean also makes this portrait, an art of attraction which visitors and residents are blessed to have and keep the picture-perfect frame. Washington State's biggest city is Seattle. This is a seaport city. The Puget Sound region where I live, is home to Seattle as well as other cities including Olympia, Tacoma, Everett, Port Townsend, and Bremerton. Life here is framed by the beautiful nature and its true glory.

Seattle, like much of this country, was previously inhabited by the Native Americans. The name Seattle derives from Chief Si'ahl, who is also known as Chief Seattle. We still have the Native American population struggling to preserve their amazing ancestral history.

My father, an American man with a European background, was six feet tall and very broad. He had golden blond hair and ocean blue eyes. I did not get his looks yet I was a proud daughter of a very elegant man. My father had retold a famous historical story to me about a cabinetmaker named Jonathan Edward Back. It is said Mr. Back had accidently caused a fire after toppling a glue pot. After the incident, however, he tried to extinguish the fire with water, which then caused the burning glue to increase even further.

The great fire of Seattle is a gloomy historical true story known to all her residents, as this had pointblank scorched thirty-one blocks. The present-day Downtown Seattle was fashioned again, on top of the previously existing city. Today, the tour guides will walk you down the horrific memory lanes of the past inhabitants and their homes as they retell the stories of the past.

The Seattle underground was exhibited in several movies. I loved watching these movies as this is my father's birthland. This underground is also known for famous ghostly sightings and it became famous for ghost hunters.

My grandmother's house is in the Seattle metropolitan area with the beautiful Puget Sound drifting by uniting land and water. Tacoma has her own history and is known for the picturesque historical architecture and her historical homes. Again, ghost stories and paranormal stories of their own brew here too. The famous Thornewood Castle is also nearby, located in Lakewood. Thornewood Castle was the set of the fictional Stephen King TV series Rose Red and has seen various paranormal activities. I loved reading about all these stories as these cities have so much beauty, mystery, and romance in common. The Creator has created a mysterious land with stories from the past to the present for the future.

My father said it very simply. His hometown has her own thrills as she serves all her guests, long-term or short-term. Within her chest, she has the best coffee shops as Starbucks was born here, the famous century-old farmer's market also known as Pike Place Market, the Space Needle, and amongst all, the paranormal activities. In her chest, Washington State, like her famous coffee and fresh baked bread, welcomes all race, color, and religion as she places them in one bowl and spreads all throughout the land. A beautiful picture is then formed in the canvas of an author like me.

I watched my father, Dr. Andrew Newhouse, was so happy to be here after all his travels even though he was devastated inside as he just lost his father. Yet somehow I think he was praying he would find his father sitting on the porch of his family home to welcome him. He knew this was his home. Every time he would land here, he would take a deep breath and say, "Home at last." This is where he had always come back to after all of his travels, for within her chest, he found peace.

It was a long journey from India to Seattle, Washington. I was so excited as for the first time, I was visiting my paternal grandmother whom I had never seen. My mother, Dr. Gita Shankar Newhouse, an Indian woman, five feet and two inches tall, with olive skin, long raven black hair, and brown eyes, was the beauty queen of her hometown. She and my father had met on a working medical journey to Africa. Both doctors volunteered to save the children throughout the globe.

They went from country to country treating all humans for they both believed in the humanitarian acts of kindness more than the war that drives us apart. Against the will of their families, they married and lived worldwide, a place they both found peace within.

My maternal grandparents accepted my father and had a blessed time as my father and mother let religion not tear them apart. They respected both, my father – a Catholic, and my mother – a Hindu. After years of not getting in touch, finally my paternal grandmother called upon us. The news, however, was a tragic event. She called her estranged son and told all of us with broken sobs, my paternal grandfather, Martin Newhouse, had passed away. We were flying over to be by her side as even though she rejected the union of my parents, they all wanted to be there with her and for her.

I am an only child. While my parents went on their journey of saving the world, I was left with my maternal grandparents. I thought my parents were strangers to me just like my paternal grandmother would be. I stayed quiet on the long plane ride even though I missed my Nana, Hari Shankar, and Nani, Parvati Shankar.

Hindi was my first language as taught to me by my maternal grandparents. My only family, my only home, through my entire childhood and now as a grown-up, was my maternal grandparents. My parents had visited me on their routes to and from work. I was their vacation stopover. I never got to bond with them. As a child, I always thought they were guests visiting.

Not very used to plane rides unlike my parents, I slept all the way. We had flown into California and were going to take the bus from Los Angeles to Seattle. My parents thought of always taking the hardest route to and from while flying, never the easiest, as we could have come to Seattle-Tacoma International Airport but they chose the other route.

I heard a lot about my grandmother and Seattle. As my father had all his untold stories hidden in his chest, I never thought how much he missed his family, his home, or his friends, but he reminded me always that for his love, he would give up all of this in a blink again. I knew he would give it all up for his love.

It was amazing just to watch them, the lovebirds. They always held on to one another and devoted their lives to saving the children all around the globe. Even to this day, they held on to each other throughout the plane ride and even on the bus. I watched my parents considering each other's eyes, as newlyweds would watch one another. They were always watching one another even as they had conversations with others.

I loved this aspect of my parents. Yet I wondered what kind of a mother I would be. I would never let him, my child be alone, for I would never let go of the father or the child. I want to raise my own child if I get the chance and maybe travel together, if I could only find them.

My parents kept me safe and away from their life of giving so I could have a stable life. I wished they had not done that so I could have witnessed this wonderful love story firsthand. I felt lucky to have been a child from this blessed union. Yet I felt deprived from being held by them because they loved me. For love, they kept me away. Yet for love, I wanted to be with them.

I was watching an old woman give me weird stares for a while as we had boarded the bus. She watched me without a blink. The woman seemed to be from another era or something as she was clothed in olden day getup. She was very elegant and had an aura to her complete being. I kept on thinking about the Little House on the Prairie TV series and thought she jumped out of it, or rather an old witch movie set.

I leaned near my father as he too watched her. She said, "You have a nice family. I am Marinda, a seer, and I have traveled from the sixteenth century."

My father replied, "Yes, I do have a blessed family and right now we are traveling back home from India."

The woman kept on staring at me as she said, "Your parents are unique and different. It proves all race, color, and religion can unite for love."

I was happy at this and replied, "Yes I know, and I am lucky."

She watched my mother and said, "This stranger prays for your daughter, for your child will find love in a unique situation. I hope and again pray she is able to endure all of what this life is blessing, or some may say cursing, her with. She too has traveled time and is fighting with her destiny to be with him and not away from him."

She continued watching my mother and said, "I wish you two had altered your ways of raising your only child, as she will be lonely and be left without you to be by her side again. It is strange you trained her to grow up alone as she must be alone by herself once again. Maybe it is better this way, but I also think whatever time we all have, we should be with one another and at least try to be a family."

My mother was now holding on to my father who sat in between us trying to hold on to me. My mother just shook her head as she did not know what to say.

The woman continued, "Do you believe in fate and destiny? Do pray for your child as I tell you, her twin flame is different, very different. He is from a different time or a different place and land. They must have strong faith to find one another. He was born at the same time, yet he searches for her through the mist, and thinks of her past life face and yet does not see her this life face."

She watched me and said, "I pray dear child, your son, an amazing noble child, be able to guide and unite you with your twin flame. The union between you two will have to rip worlds apart. Two souls must cross the Earth and beyond as the unknown and known reality must open a door for this union."

She looked out the window and again said, "Your twin flame must accept you, believe in you, and awaken himself to this reality. He must walk through the door of dreams as he was born in a Christian family. Remember my words. When life gives you pain and struggles, it is then you must be strong and not give up on your dreams."

She watched me and said, "Remember enduring pain is a struggle between the human body and the inner soul. Please remember my words, 'Physical pain treated through medication, emotional pain treated through meditation.' You two shall meet yet you must remember, time past must be kept in a sacred place for only then the union shall be. The past and the present shall create the future. Also, never awaken a sleepy soul or a dreamer unless he is ready."

I watched her as she said, "Your dreams will guide you to him as he will also find you, but his dream girl standing in front of him might not be what he thinks of her or how he sees her. It is then you must wait. Never awaken a dreamy person with the truth unless he too awakens and knows of you."

Our bus shattered as we saw there was a huge truck coming from the opposite side. In the next scene, all I remember is there was no air and I could not breathe. Water was all around me. As I felt the terrible pain in my chest, I knew I was suffocating and all I could see was light.

I thought, so is this how it feels to die? Or am I in the tunnel of reincarnation or rebirth, for all I feel is nothing? I thought but my parents are doctors, so why are they not doing anything?

I kept on reciting the Mahāmrityunjaya Mantra. I also recited Hail Mary, Our Father, and one Act of Contrition.

I remembered my mother saying, "Always the last hope, call upon the motherland or the land your feet walks upon for she always holds the ultimate healing powers. The land beneath your feet shelters all humans within her chest as they take birth or as their final resting shelters."

I wondered, would a land I never knew accept my prayers or my calls? I knew a mother never discriminates between her birth or adopted children. This adopted child today needs your motherly embrace, dear birthplace of my father.

So, I called upon this land and cried to her, "Please help me, oh the blessed land Seattle, guide this child who has come and landed upon your shore. Alone, lonely, and frightened my soul is, but I know within a land hides the greatest power to protect all of her children, whether they be born or adopted. May this accident not be my destiny as I know I was blessed to be destined to Seattle, Washington."

# CHAPTER THREE:

## *Eternally Yours, Vows From The Beyond*

*"My beloved, this weak heart only beats eternally for you. Through life or even in death, this mind, body, and soul are, were, and shall always be yours for eternity."*

*Erasmus van Phillip belongs only to Anadhi Newhouse or was it Anant belongs only to Amara? Who was here saving her as he uttered his eternal vows from the beyond?*

The water was freezing. It felt like a sharp knife piercing through my skin as all around I could see nothing but water. I was breathing but felt nothing. My whole body felt like rubber. I wondered if I could control my body or not. I was able to think and contemplated if I was dreaming. Do I just wake up and run to my Nani? I wondered where Mother was. I needed her now. Where was Father? I needed him now.

I pondered why I had worn a white, sexy gown on my bus trip as it felt weird. My mother had always dressed me up like a princess and had wanted to see me wearing this gown when my grandmother had first seen me. Strangely, I started to laugh as my maternal grandparents taught me to call my parents, "Mother and Father" for they did not know English, but just the basic words.

I thought my parents would love to hear me call them in English, so I call them "Mother and Father" and somehow, I could not change it as I had grown up. I was laughing aloud and thought I would choke as I swallowed water. I tried to call out to them but could not get any response from them.

I felt cold and wet but could not move. I knew I was drowning and yet I felt peace and blessings around me. I felt my mother's belief in Lord Shiva, her mother's belief in

Lord Krishna, and as I heard the chanting of Hindu prayers, I also saw the light and knew the Holy Spirit was watching over me as I heard my father's Catholic belief all around me. I saw angels watching over as I heard my father's voice reciting the Holy Rosary over me.

I woke up as I saw a man carrying me in his arms asking if I was okay. I thought the water felt so warm on this cold freezing February morning. I knew we were traveling, and Father had said it's cold in Seattle, so we had packed for the weather.

I had no clue how I ended up in this man's arms, but only that his body was warm and all I wanted to do was go back to sleep.

He said, "Hey Seattle Princess, stay awake if you can, okay? You are a true beauty and so sexy I could watch over you eternally."

Who was this man talking into my ears? Whispers from a stranger are dangerous. My Indian grandmother would say run away from him and never glare into his eyes. I did just the opposite of what I was taught and gazed right into his eyes. He smiled as if he knew exactly what I was thinking.

He laughed out loud. His voice was so mesmerizing. I wanted to forget everything that I just might be dying and wanted to only listen to his voice. I watched him like a lovestruck woman who saw her love for the first time. He was tall about six feet, five inches. His eyes were gray-blue and his hair was light brown. He had a French beard and within my eyes, he looked like a Greek god or something.

He had a white shirt on and it was open in the front, maybe a fashion statement. My unsteady mind kept on telling me he must have been an artist or maybe a model from a portrait who just walked out of it. He had an antique pocket watch on his wrist wrapped around saying he traveled time just for me.

He asked, "Do you fear me? If you want, I can leave you in this water, but I really think it's my duty to save a human in distress. Specially a woman, who pulls me to her with her beautiful vows of the beyond."

I was trying to understand what he was talking about. Where were my parents and that old woman from the bus? I still remember her words stinging in my ears. Some words never leave you and these words of the unknown face will stay with me forever.

I felt something different about this man as I opened my eyes and realized he was walking over water or was he floating, I could not tell. I wanted to scream and jump but somehow I was unable to move. I felt numb inside and outside. I thought okay, an angel, he must be an angel.

How lucky I must be. This angel was so handsome. I was going crazy thinking where these thoughts were coming from. I wanted him to hold on to me forever.

I asked him, "Who are you, and are you from this Earth, this time, or beyond?"

He watched me in shock and somehow I wondered was he hurt as he looked like he too was in pain, yet he never complained.

He said, "I am not from the beyond but from Earth, actually a land called the Netherlands."

I heard him and thought he said what? Did he say he was Peter Pan from Neverland?

He asked, "Why are you scared of me? Your parents must have taught you some prayers to protect you from all evil, right? I assure you I am not evil. Truth is I don't know how I am here and if this is a dream or not. But I am enjoying holding on to you as much as you love being held."

I was thinking be a dream or anything, just don't be evil. I kept on thinking is he evil then? How does being in his arms at the time of death feel so good, so nice, and feel so right?

I wondered why it felt like I should always be in these arms. Our eyes kept locked on to one another's and I knew he was feeling the same way I was.

I thought about all the prayers my parents recited over the years but could not come up with one, so I started to recite whatever came to my mind, and it was the first time words came from my lips.

I said, "My Lord, protect me from Satan and all evil. Let no evil enter me or my heart at any time. I rest my faith in you as I rest my soul on this Earthly bed, with complete faith my Lord."

He said, "Amen."

I watched him and saw his eyes again and knew whoever he was or whatever he was, I could trust him. He heard me mind to mind, how strange. I knew I heard him as he heard me and both of us felt the strange bond of union between us.

I was watching his eyes as he was watching mine. I felt this strange feeling, let time stop and forget everything but just don't leave me. I prayed not for me but for him. I started to cry and just held on to him as if I had known him for ages. Life was nothing and death was a blessing if I could die in his embrace. I grabbed his shoulders as he held on to me without a word.

He said, "May my love awaken you and may you be safe and healthy. I will cross over Heaven and Earth for you, if only the Lord wills. I will give all that I have only to you. Always know for you I live and for you I breathe. Forever my eternal love, forever I shall protect you. Time is nothing and there is no pain that I won't cross for you. Live for me, and each and every day, pray for our complete union. Always know, my mind, body, and soul belong to you my twin flame."

His words were getting fuzzy as he still spoke but this time, he uttered in a strange tongue, a language not familiar to me, yet I understood all his words as they reached my ears.

He said, "Until our paths unite again my sweetheart, I wait for you every day and every night. Everyone shall say and think what I say is unreal but my love, please know this, my soul knows it's all true. Every breath I take is for you and every awakened or sleeping moment this blessed body is, I belong only to you."

I cried and told him, "Never let me go. Promise me you will forever hold on to me."

He said, "Life has given me this test I take every day. I live time after time only to awaken and find my bed is empty as you are missing. My dreams are of you and I live all day thinking only of you. Life holds still as my love I only live for you. Never give up and keep on fighting for we shall unite. Time and tide won't keep us apart. The ocean knows of our love story. The skies are witnesses to this love story. Time flies by and life passes by but remember I shall always be waiting for you."

I cried again as I repeated, "Never let go of me! I don't care if I am dead or alive. I just want to be with you. Keep me in your heart. Promise forever you are only mine."

He cried as he kissed my lips and said, "I shall rip the skies open and find you. Forever and ever, you are mine and only mine, from my soul to your soul from your soul to mine. May this union be, from heavens above and Earth beneath. May my love for you and your love for me tie us eternally in a union for eternity. Remember my love, eternally yours, vows from the beyond."

# CHAPTER FOUR:

## *Grandmother's Embrace*

*"Relationships are created at birth without choice yet shattered or recreated through the journey of life by choice."*

*Anadhi Newhouse woke up from a coma to find out her heart still beats to be within the embrace of a grandmother whom she did not even know.*

I could feel the gentle traces of his hands all over my hair as he kept on asking me to never forget him. His words were loud and clear as he repeated, "Anadhi, my Ana, please wait for me and promise you will fight for me as I promise to fight for you. Promise in life or in death, you are mine."

I called him and asked him not to leave me. I kept on saying, "Eras, Erasmus, please don't let go of me. If my dream breaks, and I don't have you anymore, I feel lonesome again."

I woke up on a hospital bed. The smells and sounds of hospitals always made me sick even though I was used to going to work with my parents when they took me with them. They lived their whole lives treating patients. The hospital was their first home. Personally, I stayed far away from any hospital if I could. My Nana and Nani loved hospitals as they would talk to everyone about how their daughter was educated and became a famous doctor. Everyone in their serene village knew about her.

It was a dark room except the monitors all around me were blinking yellow, green, and red lights. I had an IV and heart monitor and my fingers had oxygen monitors on them as well. There was a TV on the wall and a recliner with an elegant elderly European woman snoring next to me.

I had no clue where I was and who she was. I wanted to push the nurse button but couldn't reach as it was tucked away on the wall. I should've screamed for help and seen if anyone would come, but it's just that the woman in the recliner looked so uncomfortable yet so comfortable sleeping and I had no heart to wake her up.

I wanted my mother or father to walk in and take me home. They could just take care of me at home. I didn't want to be here. Without knowing, I started to talk in Hindi as I did with my mother and called out for her, "Mother."

I saw the older woman jerk up. She immediately pressed the help button and started to scream, "Help someone! Help! My granddaughter is awake. Please someone come on and save her. Please don't let another death be. I can't take it anymore! Have I not been cursed enough? My Lord, please guide me and save the last of my bloodline!"

I was shocked, as to what was she talking about and who was she? The door opened and I saw doctors and nurses walk in calmly and comfortable as always for they must see these kinds of activities every day.

A doctor said, "Hi, How are you? I am Dr. Zhang, Jonathan Zhang. This is Agatha Newhouse. Sister Agatha is your nurse and a nun from the church. I know you are not familiar with her, but she is also your father's paternal aunt."

I asked, "Where are my parents? Are they not here? I want to speak to them first."

The doctor looked like a Chinese-American biracial doctor. I was happy to see another biracial person like me. I watched the nurse who also came in. She was an elderly woman of European background. She had golden blonde hair like my father and her complexion too was similar to him. Her eyes watched me like his eyes would. I wondered why she reminded me of him.

The doctor avoided my questions and just checked on me. As he did, he avoided eye contact and asked, "What do you remember last? How did you end up in the Puget Sound near Chambers Bay in University Place, near Tacoma, Washington?"

He continued to say, "You are one lucky woman. Your ID and passport were intact in your bag. Your grandmother kept on looking for you and had sent your pictures to all the local police stations."

I was confused and realized the doctor was interrupted by the elderly woman as she thought he should stop talking. She said in her authoritative voice, "Thank you Dr. Zhang but I can handle the details of my granddaughter as you can handle only her physical condition."

I remember trying to stay awake but all I remember were words coming from far away. As the words started to fade away, I only saw the face of another man who was not even in this room but kept on asking, "Baby, can you hear me?"

He said again, "Sweetheart, please fight for me as in this life we must unite somehow, some way. Breaking all the barriers, we have to unite. Please for me live and wake up. I love you today, tomorrow, and yesterday. I love you eternally. Forever, I love you."

I wanted to hear the voice again and again and hold on to his hands. As I was holding on to his hands for the life of my soul, I jerked open my eyes and I saw a woman rubbing my hands.

She said, "Strong hands. You have a good grip and are getting stronger. How does it feel to be home?"

I saw everything clear as I sat up and she said, "You have been in and out for a long time, but this is it. You have recovered and now are out of danger."

I asked, "What danger?"

As she let go of my hands and opened the windows, I saw rain pouring hard outside. The winds were singing musical tunes of the falling rain. It felt like true lovers were dancing in the rain. I love the rain. I was distracted as I wanted to just go outside and watch the rain and the Earth so lovingly dance together as if they were long-lost lovers and missed each other for so long. I felt finally they have united. Let them be together, completely in love.

Again, I remembered the unknown face of the unknown man I called Erasmus. Somehow my whole inside felt it was missing the beats of life as I missed him more than I wanted to admit to anyone. I wondered who he was that he had taken away my inner control, my peace.

I came back to reality as the rain poured in even heavier than before. With each drop, I could hear the anklets of Earth and the flute of rain. It's an amazing sound as the winds join in with joy, the lighting, and the thunder also can't stay away for they know after a long separation, this couple has united. They are announcing to the universe, let's all celebrate this union. I saw there was a sliding door in this room and a beautiful porch outside.

I remembered him and wanted to go back to where he was, my angel in disguise. My heart cried out for him as if I had known him for ages from another birth or was it from heavens above? I packed my emotions on hold and knew I must stand up on my feet first, then find him. The tears that started to fall for the unknown stranger, I had to swallow back into my eyes and get back to reality.

I knew I was not in the hospital anymore. How and when I got here, I had so many questions to ask her, but I knew I must stay awake for all of these answers. I wanted to go back to sleep just to see him once more.

Who is he? Why do I remember him? The rain and the Earth, the union of lovers all around the universe only pulled me to him, his memories, his eyes, those hands. I just wanted to go back into that dream and not wake up for my soul wanted to just be with him. Time was where all the answers laid. I must let time take me on a journey through life for all the unknown answers of life.

I thought of all these unanswered questions, yet all I had was time. There was a huge gap between my unanswered, unasked questions and all the answers. It was called time.

I sat up as the kind woman came back and helped me get up. She walked by my side. I was shocked I knew where the restroom was and all of this house was so familiar to me. She smiled and answered my questions as I came out of the restroom.

She said, "It's a shock as to why you don't remember anything yet know all of the house and where everything is. It's normal for you were in a very bad accident. With time, everything, all of it, will come back as you will wake up more normally to your surroundings. It's a weird thing. Her name is time. Sometimes it's as if she doesn't want to leave us and at times, she leaves us without giving any warnings. It's then we work with her and learn to live with her as that's our only way out. The present must walk with her as she takes us through this tunnel."

She continued, "As the days pass by, we know we can never stop time or tide, but we have this day, this time, so today, love all of this around us."

Such a beautiful phrase said so simply as it also answered my questions. I too must take what has been thrown onto my lap with kindness and not waste my days living in the past. With the passing of this day, I will lose this time by chasing after what has been lost and is in the past. It hurts a lot as I want to live in the past and bring all of it back, but how do we do what is not humanly possible? I must be strong and let this wounded warrior inside me heal for I am a warrior and all that I have with me is the present. This is a gift and I will fight until this day is no more.

Mother had taught me, "You always have this day. It ends with the human body as the body becomes ashes to ashes and all that remain from each human are memories we leave for the future generation."

I will live until my time too comes to be the future for then I become no more as I then too am but the past.

I asked her, "Who are you? Where have you come from? Please don't take this personally. May my words not hurt you for I am so confused as to who you are. Why have you been taking care of this unknown person?"

I watched an elegant patient woman just watch me and let me finish my thoughts. I told her, "Within my knowledge, we have never met and even then, you seem so close to me as if I have known you my entire life. I am a Hindu-Christian and my mother had taught me that at times even strangers seem so closely bonded as though we have known them all of our lives. It is then we seek and know we were somehow connected to each other in other lifetimes. I believe in reincarnation and my heart guides me as I let her decide."

I told her again, "I hear my father's teachings. He had taught it's okay to let your heart rule and follow the holy scriptures if we have our eyes and mind open to reality and let our thoughts conjure up and find the facts."

The very elegant woman asked me, "What do you remember? Where are you from? Tell me more about yourself as I will tell you everything about myself slowly."

I told her, "Please, don't find my words strange. I have been living in India with my grandparents who are devoted Hindus. They also taught me the teachings of meditation and the meditative soul. That is how I survived the accident I had been in, aside from a miracle. As the water drowned me, I went into a meditative state. I knew I would let my body fall into a sleeping state as known in the spiritual world and use the sound Aum to guide me back to this Earth."

I watched her for a while as she only suggested with her eyes for me to continue. I said to her, "I need to know who you are and if we are related. I believe we are somehow related. Either from the past, present, or future, we are related."

The kind woman just stood there as she rubbed her hands and said, "Yes, you are an old and very wise soul. I see that now and even when I had not known you or had not laid my eyes upon you, I knew you are mine and always were mine and always will be. It's not that I had known or not but remember even an unknown person might be the one who is and will be your family forever. Sometimes, we are born lucky and have our family all around us and at times, we find each other after a tragedy."

I saw her cheeks were covered in tears. That hurt me more than if the tears were mine. I don't know why I felt I should wipe her tears off, yet I was bound by my fears of rejection.

She watched me with the knowledge and said, "From this time on forward, I am here for you and know even in the past, my prayers were with you even though I was not."

She held her hands out for me. As I watched her eyes, I saw an elderly woman with so much strength and will had given her steady solid hands out to me.

She smiled and her kind, warm heart watched me as she said, "May my hands always be there for you. Even when you may not be there, you shall always find me here with my arms open wide. All my love I give you my dear child as I am the woman who gave birth to your father, he called me Mom. I will be there for you forever and honored if you call me Grandmother."

I watched the elderly woman who looked very independent and strong, yet I knew she needed me as much as I needed her today. I wanted to ask her, but where are my parents? What is going on? I knew I must give her time as she had given me time to heal. I wondered on the word "Grandmother" and thought how I had wanted to see her and call her "Grandmother" all of my life.

Relationships, may they be blood or not, are hard to create or break, yet I sat in front of a family member who became my world in a few hours. Again my thoughts wandered off to a very familiar face, yet I wouldn't recognize him in the daylight hours. My life he became, yet throughout this lifetime, I had never seen him. I thought how could I keep all of this inside of me? Yet, I knew this woman in front of me knew all of this somehow.

She said at that moment, "Some relationships are created from beyond our own realizations. Some are called the half of the other. Others are called blessings from the beyond as you are my blessings from the beyond."

I realized then, he must be my other half, my twin flame. I hugged this woman and realized, never did I feel better to have a family member before, especially my own grandmother.

I held tightly on to a very stern woman who too dropped all her differences and hugged me back as she kissed my head and said, "You are the only reason my heart stills beats. Promise me, you will never leave me, not until this heart beat stops."

I watched her as I told her, "Never shall I let you go for even my heartbeats tell me, I am within my grandmother's embrace."

# CHAPTER FIVE:

## *Life Is But A Day*

*"The sun rises at dawn as the sun sets at dusk, reminding all, everything that begins must end as life is but a day."*

*Anadhi Newhouse found a message left on a swing by her deceased grandfather which tied her in a bond with him and her mystical twin flame.*

The kind elderly woman took my hands in her hands as she hugged me and said, "I am the happiest woman alive. I have you awake and alive. To have a chance to have you, hold on to you, see you breathe, and wake up is the biggest blessing of the Lord. Please give me some time as all shall be clear soon."

I gave her my hands and felt how this slender, tall woman in her seventies, stood tall and strong. She smiled back as we walked to the porch and sat on a beautiful swing which hung from the ceiling of the covered porch. I had not wanted to ask anything as from an Indian background, I was taught never to interrupt elders when they are talking.

Let time pass on by as she will smooth out any space you have in between each other. For if time was who took away all the memories from you, then it is she, who will return them to you in due time. In the meantime, be patient.

My grandmother watched me as she said, "Your grandfather had this swing built for us days before he passed away. He had said it was a gift for your mother to give to you. Even though he knew he will never see her, he knew one day you will come and sit on this swing as the breeze will blow your beautiful black hair and he will have peace.

He even imprinted the name Anant meaning 'infinite' on it for you. Why Anant, you might wonder, but in time you shall know."

I knew then this woman is my grandmother. She is just like Father without saying directly who she is, she just did. Why was I hearing what was going on? I knew from all around something must be wrong, very wrong. I thought my name Anadhi also means infinite. I wondered why he had my name yet a different version of it written on the swing.

She continued as she knew I was holding on to every word. I was trying to be positive and keep my calm. I also am my father's daughter as I heard Mother say so many times.

Grandmother said, "I am trying to give you all of the truth without leaving anything out but it's hard. I just buried three members of my family, your grandfather, your father, and your mother."

I felt everything all around me went dark as the only thing I saw was a woman whom I never met in my life say my parents were no more. I must be strong for I saw I did not die from this news but just sat there next to this stranger who also was sitting next to me very much alive.

We both were bonded in union by tragedy. No words could bring any solace or peace for as my ears had heard the truth, I had realized I had known the truth. In my heart, I had died with my parents and I wanted to go back to India for maybe then all would go back to normal. Maybe my parents were waiting for me in India. I must go back and find them.

I felt her hands hold on to my hands and say, "My sweet granddaughter, may I be there for you. Our paths cross at this obstacle of life, for she is the biggest mountain we have to cross. May I have you and your hands to help me walk over this mountain. Life brings us together at the door of death, but may you be my walking stick as I shall be yours if you have me."

I saw her words had brought tears to my eyes not at the words of death but of life, a person asking for help to deal with the hardship of life, not to deal with the loss of life. I nodded and told her I will be there for her always. Without saying anything, I let my tears roll and I knew my calmness was not obeyed by my abandoned tears, which had left the inner ocean of my eyes and flooded my vision. For always, my tears have deceived me.

She hugged me and told me people waste life living in anger and misery as she did too. Now she prefers to live life in joy and giving in laughter and sorrow, not waste time on anger for time lost is gone like the wind and shall never come back.

That night as we sat on the porch watching the stars appear in the night skies, we both looked up and wondered if our family members were like stars blinking in the sky. I found out no one survived the bus accident except for me. The bus had fallen into the Puget Sound and all lives were lost in the dark night. The bus was recovered with all dead, leaving one missing. How I ended up so far away from Seattle, no one knows but it was strange as if someone picked me up and landed me upon my grandmother's doorstep. I was found within a five minutes' walk away from her house.

I held on to my grandmother as I knew we look so different. I am petite with an olive complexion and I have long black hair with dark brown eyes. My grandmother is a tall European woman with brown hair and green eyes. Yet we are so similar as she said I reminded her of her son. I knew what she was saying for even though my grandmother was sitting next to me, I felt Father was looking at me through those eyes they both share that are so alike.

She asked me, "Do you remember anything from the night?"

I said, "Yes, those eyes of that man. He has gray-blue eyes. I remember him carrying me over water, and as he laid me down, he had said until we meet again to fight and stay alive for him."

I remember his eyes. I thought why it was I only see the eyes of a person as if it gives me the depth of a person's soul. I can see into the person deep below the inner soul only by considering the eyes. I could see the eyes and foretell people's future until my Nani in India told me not to share this as people might think I am a witch or something.

I also told my grandmother, "I can't remember but I think the man who saved me said he was from Neverland. Grandmother, I thought he was Peter Pan."

She just watched me and was in her own world thinking about who the kindhearted Samaritan that saved me was. Sometimes I wonder how did I land upon this woman's doorstep? Was this a coincidence or something mysterious? I retold to her all I could remember about my dream man. I watched my grandmother just watch me as if this was so normal and she knew exactly what I was saying.

She said, "One day, I will talk about my forefathers who have come from a faraway land, called the Netherlands. Maybe he said the Netherlands. Maybe all of this will make more sense in the future, but until then we must find a way to live and let time guide us."

I laughed as I told her, "You remind me of my maternal grandmother and her wise words about time and healing."

She laughed and said, "It's the only thing that connects all humans to one another, known to all as the healing mantra called time. Also, I must meet your other grandmother as we have the love of our life, you, in common."

Time had passed by us as she waits for none. Today she has made a path for my grandmother and me to unite under this umbrella of a family. Today we have this time for something. I wondered what my destiny in life is. Why have I landed here? Who is that man and why does he appear in my dreams and now I see him even during the day?

My questions piled up as I thought who I was, for how I could foretell the future? I could also heal people. How and why then did I not even see the end of my parents, or was it that I refused to see? I knew I must stand up on my feet and recall my own memories first, then all shall come back to me. I must also open the door of reincarnation for even more answers.

All this I kept in my chest for so long and now I knew I must awaken for my mother's words kept coming back to my ears as she had repeated all of her life, "Live life to the fullest. Do your share as a creation of the Creator and always remember no tears at the end of this life journey as life is but a day."

I must live this day and beyond to find out who was the man that had taken my heart away with his vows from the beyond. I realized Mother wanted me to live my life to the fullest and all the days I do live, compare it to a day. As nightfall approached and sleep had taken over my soul, again I saw him. Yet this was a strange dream.

I saw two children around five years old, yet the girl looked much younger than the boy. I knew I was the young girl and my mystery man was the young boy. The strangest part was I called him Anant as he called me Amara.

I cried and told him, "Anant, don't leave me! I'm scared!"

I cried as I was running through a forest and knew I must find a clearing. I could barely see anything as it was a dark and heavily forested area. I knew I must find Anant somehow as I kept calling him. There was a strange fear gripping my entire being as this kind of fear should not even be known to a young child.

I cried as I could see tears pouring out and little whimpers became loud sobs. A hand caught on to me as he placed his little hands on my mouth and asked me not to make any sounds. I saw then we walked to a clearing where the moon was shining on us and a lagoon was nearby. He told me we must jump into the river. I wanted to tell him, but I cannot swim, yet I remained quiet. I knew Anant was here so I would be fine.

I asked him, "Anant, why do people think I am a witch, because I wish I was, but I am not. If I was a witch, I would burn down all evil from this world."

He told me, "It is because you are white with gray-blue eyes and have brown hair but were raised by nuns yet even they don't know where you came from. Everyone worries where you came from and why you were left behind like an orphan."

I told him, "Why am I different? I want to be like you. I don't like being an orphan. I want to have a family like you."

I wondered what had happened to my family. I also remembered my father and mother were different from a lot of people. Rumors were, they were burned at the stakes as they were accused of being witches and my father had to die because he refused to let go of his beloved wife whom everyone called a witch. Yet I knew all of these were rumors as I was an orphan.

We were in a time period when witch burnings were regular dangers all women with some special gift feared and lived with. Anant knew and wondered what had happened to my entire family. At that time, I heard footsteps and Anant told me to jump with him as I did, and we fell down a waterfall into the huge lagoon. All I could remember was trying to find Anant.

I woke up crying and repeating, "Anant, don't leave me, I can't swim."

My grandmother had come into my room as she asked what was going on. I told her I had a dream and thought I was in the time period when everyone was practicing witch burnings. I told her I was white, and

Erasmus was Anant as he was Indian. My grandmother hugged me as she told me to walk with her to the back porch as she wanted to share a story and show me something.

I sat on the same swing and saw the Anant name inscribed on the swing.

I asked her, "How did you know?"

She replied, "Your grandfather was positive we were having a grandson who would be named Anant. Yet when we had a granddaughter, he shared his dreams of Anant and how we must find Anant, yet it is hard as he has changed and is different now. So, he inscribed Anant for all to have when we would need it. Yes, your grandfather had told me he too had seen Anant as Erasmus. Even he was confused, so we just let it go."

I cried as I touched the swing and knew Grandfather never believed in reincarnation, yet I thought he must have. I wondered what we should do now, and how does life go on like this? I asked him mind to mind, what am I to do now, Anant? Who are you now?

My grandmother said, "We live life. We should all take a vacation and travel the world, and maybe go to the mystical lands of this Earth. For my dear child do remember, life is but a day."

# CHAPTER SIX:

## *Land Of Mystery, India*

*"Where the mystical skies pour fragrances of love in the air, where rivers bathe pure essence into the lives of all, where heavenly love ties humans into a bond of humanity, is in one word, blessed India."*

*Symbol of love, the Taj Mahal in India, had pulled
Anadhi Newhouse, giving her a message not to give up
on her love and the vows from the beyond.*

**S**ound of the doorbell awakened me from my daydreams as I heard Aunt Agatha say, "I know Miranda, you are here and so are you Anadhi."

We both laughed as I went and hugged Aunt Agatha. Grandmother told her, "When has a closed door kept you out?"

A nurse, a nun, and an herbalist, some call her a modern-day witch with magical powers. She laughed as she hugged me and I knew all the magical therapies I had received from Aunt Agatha helped with the back pain I had suffered from the accident. Aunt Agatha had in her picnic basket, mint, lavender, oregano, basil, sage, and a loaf of bread.

She watched me as I was looking at her and told her, "I have to share a memory from the bus accident. I had not shared with anyone as it had bothered me for days and still haunts me to this day."

They both said nothing as we all sat for breakfast. I had my coffee as they were drinking homemade herbal tea. How close I had become with these relatives of mine and knew they would not say anything until I was ready to share.

I was emotionally and physically torn between the disbelief of my parents' death and the visions of my dream man whom I had seen every day and night since my accident. The dreams were also shared by my grandmother and Aunt Agatha. They had spent restless nights as they visited the dreamlands where there was this man who was always sitting with us living in a paranormal life where nothing was frightening but all was a fairytale love story.

The whole family was having interlinking dreams where a man calls upon all of us to help find him. I wished we could all somehow find him yet thought how would this be possible in reality.

Aunt Agatha started talking, "I have done my research and looked up a lot of people who were involved in near-death experiences. Some remember the tunnel of light and some don't, yet some become psychic."

I asked her, "What about the interlinking dreams we are all having? I saw Erasmus and you all have seen him even before I did. Grandfather had seen him as Anant, proving the reincarnation theory."

Aunt Agatha continued, "I found a few interesting books on dreams and the theories about reincarnation, twin flames, and much more as I found an author named Ann

Marie Ruby. I brought her books along for all of you to read and let us agree miracles from the beyond are just that, miracles. We all shall have faith in our own dreams and the interlinking dreams, like Ann Marie says she believes if a few people in the same household see roughly the same dream or reoccurring dreams, then the Lord is asking us to investigate. She also says do not get lost in your dreamland but let the dreams take their own course."

My grandmother said at that time, "Let us do some traveling, maybe traveling will help and guide us. I am old and it is time I see the world through my own eyes. Also, I believe sometimes one must walk upon the land to awaken to her past lives she had lived within that land."

We had decided to take a trip to the land of my mother as I was taking too long to heal. The two newfound loves of my life wanted to take a trip to India, they called the land of healers, I called the land of spices. Together, we all traveled to the mystical land of rebirth, as we finally agreed to call this land, the mystical and magical land.

India is a country in South Asia known for beauty and diversity as different religions have taken birth throughout time. The name India originated from Indus which also derived from the word Hindu, an old Persian term which was a prehistoric name for the Indus River. Indians were signified to as citizens of the Indus by primeval civilizations such as the Greeks.

Mythology becomes alive as even with time, the Hindu deities stand tall as their presence still is felt all over this mystical land. One of the oldest holy scriptures, known as the Vedas, were composed during 1500 to 500 BCE. Meditation or Dhyana is also linked to this time period of Hinduism. During the seventh century, Islam also landed upon this land.

We had arrived at Indira Gandhi International Airport in New Delhi, where we met our tour guide, a devoted Hindu. My maternal grandparents lived in a remote village near Agra where the famous Taj Mahal stands as a signature of love. I had visited the grand site also known as the place of eternal love, quite a few times throughout my life.

As we all entered the great Taj, we wondered would we get some kind of memory flashes here but nothing happened. My grandmother and Aunt Agatha had spent days wondering how the Taj Mahal gave them an unhappy yet an amazing feeling. A love story, however it ends, always keeps on making its own history throughout time.

I wandered off to the charm of this mystical land. I knew as these women had taken their sightseeing tour with the guide through India, each week they went to different places. I stayed behind at my Nana's home in a village about two hours away from New Delhi.

His home is like a bungalow made from brick and mortar. It has a tin roof, a beautiful veranda, and beautiful exotic flowers blooming all around. A vegetable garden provides all the vegetables year-round as they are vegetarians.

My Nani is a shy woman who dresses in complete Indian attire and loves to cook for her family from abroad. Aunt Agatha and Grandmother Miranda loved their kindhearted welcome invitation and lived together in this bungalow where there was no TV or entertainment other than the villagers and their welcoming hearts.

The afternoon hot chai time was very much appreciated as the villagers always arrived to have chai and talk until dusk. The bungalow had open windows through which one could see the huge pond, where people would come to do evening prayers. I watched Muslims and Hindus talk and walk side by side as neighbors helped out one another.

I felt my two beautiful women all dressed in local attire were born there as they wandered through this exotic land of wonder in search of solace to seek answers to our lonely hearts. Grandmother Miranda and Aunt Agatha had traveled to all different temples to find answers to our unasked questions.

Our village home is very close to where I could see the Ganges River flow. It is a magical place where one could see the Ganges flowing as far as the eyes could see. I spent my days here as I watched pilgrims taking a dip into the water and purify themselves. Every day, there would be new pilgrims wandering for peace and support from the Gods as if to give a vision. I spent days in my maternal grandparents' village home.

As I watched the Ganges River, I again had my dreams enter and take me on a different kind of adventure. This night's dream again felt so realistic. I had found another kind of love awaken within my mind, body, and soul I thought could not be possible, yet it was born within my inner soul.

Everything was dark as I was trying to jump into the Ganges River. I saw again I was a child and Anant was with me jumping ahead of me. I cried and screamed his name, "Anant! Help! I am scared!"

Anant screamed back, "Amara, I have you, hold on to me as I have you!"

He then told me to remember, "Anant Amara, Amara Anant."

I knew our names meant Infinite Love and Love Infinite. As I saw Anant's hand had caught on to me and said he had me and not to worry, the dream shifted.

I was swimming alone now. Anant was nowhere near me and I knew I was swimming from the Himalayas to Varanasi through the Ganges River. How I knew was also strange as I heard throughout my dream, people were singing, "Har Har Gange."

I was tired and thirsty even though I was in the Ganges River. I cried and saw I was floating on top of my mother, yet I knew she was not my mother. She told me not to worry as the Ganges River will take me to the land, I need to be in.

Then again I saw my dream shifted and still through the body of the Ganges, I was swimming. I was now walking through the riverbank as now I was running as an adult and

I had held on to the hands of a young boy. The skies were roaring above us and the long journey had both of us tired and hungry for food.

We had stopped along the way as I watched the young boy work and carry people's things to get little money. He told me not to worry as he will help. He called me over and over again. With shock, I tried to listen to this young child around seven years old call me "Mama."

He said, "Mama, we are almost in Bengal, as we followed the Ganges River, but we need to go and take a cab to 98467."

I watched the young boy and asked, "Where is Papa?"

My son replied, "In the land of tulips, Papa resides, but we must go to this land and then we will go and find Papa."

Then I saw my son had given me the cold drink of water I was so thirsty for as we began to run again and this time I had held on to the little hands of my son. I watched how we had journeyed through the complete path of the Ganges River and flew into a yellow cab that had the number written on it. My young boy had stayed hidden within my womb all along as he had said he wanted to hide inside of my cloak.

My dream broke as I had looked up the numbers and I talked with my grandmother next. The numbers were of a ZIP Code near Seattle. For the first time in my life, I had cried for a child I have never seen or held yet all of my heart belonged to him after his father.

How could this be real and why was this happening to me? One dark night, I had become a mother to a child yet before dawn broke open, I am a lonely single woman. Yet why then does my inner soul miss this unknown child to whom I have given my complete love?

Where and how do I find you my child? Within the dark nights, you came to me like a glowing star of hope. I know you shall guide me as the biggest sun on Earth breaks through and gives us daylight.

I needed to spend more time studying the Hindu religion through this land. I had spent my time with my Nana who had found peace at a complex of temples the villagers had created themselves. In the complex, there is a Lord Shiva temple, a Goddess Kali temple, and a Lord Hanuman temple.

I spent days praying to the Gods of this mystical land as to guide me and show me where am I to go and what to do so that my life could bring me back what I have lost. My Nana had come with a jug of holy water from the Ganges River, as he was at the temple. He knew I was suffering yet I never told him anything.

He started to talk to me, "Life is a journey where faith is believing. I have never asked you about your faith and know you follow all different religions. Do they not say the same thing?"

I told him, "Yes, basically they all say the same thing. I also believe all religions were formed based on dreams."

He replied, "So believe in your dreams, and always follow your heart. Even though you grew up in India with us, you had stayed in boarding schools and dorms as per your parents' wishes. We have never asked you to choose a religion as your parents follow both, but have you ever gone on a Hindu pilgrimage? Hinduism identifies seven holy pilgrimage sites which are Ayodhya, Mathura, Haridwar, Varanasi, Kanchipuram, Dwarka, and Ujjain. Since you are in India, you should go and visit your mother's favorite pilgrimage place, Varanasi."

Varanasi is one of the holiest pilgrimage sites according to my mother, as this was Lord Shiva's favorite place. Whenever it was possible, my mother had visited this city. I knew I should visit this site before I leave.

Grandmother was standing by the porch as was Aunt Agatha. Both overheard our conversation and knew my trend of thought sometimes better than I would acknowledge. They both looked excited.

Grandmother told me, "We should go and visit Varanasi, call it a pilgrimage or paying respect to the residence of the religion's teacher, or abode of God. I believe the believers or non-believers all should pay their respect to this place if we are able to do so. What do you think?"

I only hugged both of them as my maternal grandmother, my Nani, came and hugged all of us.

She said in her newly learned, broken yet fluent English, "So, I shall be your guide, as you can guide all of us to the Christian pilgrimage sites next."

I knew then our journey through India will come to an end yet our travel journey to find the man from my dreams will continue with another member. I was astonished how all three women had complete faith we would find the man from my dreams in due time. Until then, we live life and learn about each other's culture and religion and all we could about the messages from the beyond.

Our trip to the pilgrimage site was an exciting yet the most sacred trip I had taken in my life. I was blessed to have my favorite travel companions with me as we toured through the mystical land of mystery, India.

# CHAPTER SEVEN:

## *Varanasi, India*

*"Pilgrims are the travelers of life, who seek, knock, and ask upon the doors of faith, searching for the answers to life's unknown fate."*

*Hope and belief in vows of the beyond had brought Anadhi Newhouse to one of the seven most holiest pilgrimage sites in Varanasi, India.*

Varanasi, India is believed to be one of the holiest pilgrimage site for Hindus, amongst the seven holy cities known as Sapta Puri, in India. Individually, these cities are known as Ayodhya, Mathura, Haridwar, Varanasi, Kanchipuram, Dwarka, and Ujjain. I researched for days on all of the sites as I had not heard about any one of them from my mother or maternal grandparents before. According to my Nana, my mother had loved visiting Varanasi, so we all started our holy pilgrimage to this sacred site.

Our hope was if we could find some answers to our questions of life. If none was found, then we would be happy with finding just inner peace. A nine-hour train ride through the most scenic places had taken us to the most astonishing sanctified site in my life. Dressed in local attire, my family and I had traveled in an air-conditioned coach class with a very friendly tour guide named Rian Ahmed, a Muslim himself, yet respected this holy site as he had taken so many pilgrims to this site. Pilgrims wanting to visit this site once in their life had been our companions.

Rian, a fluent English speaker, started to speak, "Hindu legends claim this city to be the oldest city in the world. They do claim this is around five thousand years old.

The Ganges River is framed by all kinds of old temples. All different religions are also practiced here."

I asked him, "Is this not the place where Buddhism was also founded from?"

He had taken us to the place commonly linked to the famous spot where the great Buddha had given his famous speech at.

Again Rian told us, "The great Buddha had given his famous speech, 'The Setting in Motion of the Wheel of the Dharma Sutta' here. This is a very famous and peaceful place, visited by tourists and peace seekers alike."

My family and I had participated in the holy bath, as we had taken a dip in the holy waters of the Ganges River. I watched how people were taking a dip in the Ganges River as other people were performing final funeral rites. We had stayed and enjoyed the Ganga Aarti, at sunset which is performed at every sunset by the Ganges. As I was praying, I heard a voice call and say, "Seattle Princess, wait for me."

I could not understand where the voice was coming from as the voice sounded so familiar. I remembered the same phrase was used by another person whom I barely remember but had saved me. I knew it could not be him as he was my spiritual twin flame but this person was physical.

I tried to seek him but could not see as everyone was busy with lighting diyas. I must say all the candles and the musical performances were very spiritual and I enjoyed this immensely. Here my multicultural and multireligious family sat praying for answers to something none of us could comprehend. I called this a miracle from the beyond. Yet my inner soul kept on hearing, "Seattle Princess."

Days after we had traveled back to New Delhi, I saw him again. I saw a dream and in my dream, I saw him again as this time I was walking with him over the Ganges. Then, I was in Seattle and again there was a man, an old man who had taken my hands in his hands and said, "You must go to the land of love and beauty, also known for her flowers and colors. We will meet up in Seattle. I am James. People call me the dreamer."

I told him, "We have traveled all the way to India to find my twin flame, for is this not the land of rebirth and mystery?"

I saw James showed a different land and said, "My dear child, watch."

Then again, I saw my twin flame, the mystery man as he said, "My love, find me you shall, after you find him. He is known as the dreamer, for he shall bring you to my land. There I am waiting for you and if I don't remember, please help awaken me. I know you and I will meet but promise you will be mine forever."

We had encountered mysteries as we had walked in the rural village that same day. The spiritual journey through the land of Gods known as Banaras was spiritually awakening and good for our spiritual souls.

Yet after this long day of returning home, we all saw a real-life vision. A Hindu saint had appeared from nowhere as he held on to Aunt Agatha's hand and said, "Death is an exit as birth is a re-entry for it is a traveler's journey. To know all the answers you seek, you must take help of the mystical door of dreams as through this door, you can travel without entering the doors of death."

As we sat by the Ganges River, we had witnessed a wakening miracle. A saint had conversed with us but just stopped and left. The saint talking to us, stood up and walked to the river. As he stood near the riverbank, we saw in front of us there he was sitting on an auto rickshaw and he crossed the river. His auto rickshaw had no driver yet it drove him over the water and in front of him was Seattle, Washington. After he had landed in Seattle, his auto rickshaw converted to a bridge.

Now we all saw he had landed upon a land we had never been to. We saw a land that was covered with carpets of flowers growing and dancing in the wind. Magical windmills were blowing in the wind by the canals where colorful cottages felt very welcoming.

We had all awakened to the sounds of cows roaming around us as we saw the Hindu deity Krishna's picture all around the village and knew today was a very sacred day in Hinduism as it was Janmashtami, Lord Krishna's birthday. Shaken up at the interlinking live vision we all had, yet we decided to keep this event to ourselves. We believed this was shown to us as another miracle from the beyond.

Grandmother spoke first as if reading all of our minds, "We shall all be positive and believe in these miracles as just that, miracles. We must be patient and let the miracles give us the route of our travels and know it is only time we wait for."

I knew we were just shown our traveling route, the journey that laid ahead of us. We knew all was really explained in the vision except the windmills and the colorful flowering carpets of tulips. How will all of this take place, we had no clue, yet we were all confident we shall cross this bridge as destiny takes her route.

We stayed in a village of rural India where we further educated ourselves with the theories of meditation as this is the land where meditation had taken birth as Dhyana. I talked with saints and realized religions are not different as my Catholic grandmother sits and prays for hours, so does Aunt Agatha, a Catholic nun, and my Hindu Nani. All sat and taught each other language and culture. We took support from one another as we all knew we must now return home with our acquired knowledge from India.

I kept the memories of a voice in my mind who calls me, "Seattle Princess," whom I heard again in plain daylight, in Varanasi, India.

# CHAPTER EIGHT:

## *Home Sweet Home*

*"Traveler's knowledge is gained through age-old wisdom shared throughout the lands of this Earth yet remember to share your acquired wisdom of knowledge for only then shall it forever grow."*

*Seattle became home as that's where Anadhi Newhouse found her home within the loving heart of her grandmother.*

R ainy and cloudy Seattle mornings had welcomed us back home. I felt depressed and lonely again as I came back home. The feeling was shared by my family members as we kept on hoping for more.

The regret was what if we could have solved something had we stayed for more days. Yet we were shown we must all return home. For we knew through our dreams, life will lead us to our destination but we must be the travelers.

In India, my family dressed in local attire and learned to eat Indian food, meditate, and believe in the human powers of pulling on to the good vibes. Today as we are all back home, my Nani who came along to support me through the hardest days of my life, accustomed herself to the American culture. She believes respecting all cultures without losing one's own culture is how we adapt.

We also knew we must listen to our dreams and wait in Seattle for the old wise man who shall come and visit us in his own time. So, we returned home after our long trip to India. Within our souls, we brought back with us love and mysteries from the land of mysteries.

We still enjoy Indian chai and the magical Indian food a few times a week. I know what Grandmother, Nani, and Aunt Agatha, my loving family had endured for me was like nothing one could describe within words. A life without these three would be a life in the darkness for me.

I was shocked to see they did not ever go through cultural shock. We lived near New Delhi which is known for noises, buses, taxis, and people and cows walking and sharing the same roads.

Grandmother and Aunt Agatha walked dressed in local saris as they did the shopping and visited many holy shrines of India. They loved the hospitality of everyone, from the street vendors to the taxi drivers to the hotel employees. India is an amazing magical place I lived in most of my life yet my newly found family members loved calling India their home during our mystical trip together.

I have had nightmares and dreams that made no sense. My recovery was slow as the eyes of one person followed me through time and lands. Wherever I landed, he was there.

I have this connection to him as I look for him everywhere. Sometimes I feel I will see him standing next to me in the mall. I saw him in India and in all the holy shrines I visited, he was there always like a fog.

In the fog, he told me, "Sweetheart, don't forget me as I only live for you."

In the pouring rain, he appears as he says, "By God, I want to be your umbrella as how lucky do you think the umbrella is to have you in his embrace? Now I am jealous of all the umbrellas on Earth."

My grandmother, a Catholic, who believes in all religions, and Aunt Agatha, a Catholic nun, had taken me to church as my Nani, a devoted Hindu too accompanied us. They all went to Hindu temples with me as we crossed the lands and came back home again. We walked into individual soul searching as to figure out what happened on that night in India, when we saw the Hindu saint.

I thought I must tell them about the old woman and her prediction. For unknown reasons, I did not share the event. I guess I must not completely believe it even happened as my memories are faint from just before the bus accident.

I told them, "You all know about the man who has been watching over me and know I love it that he is there. I do not know why but I feel like I am only alive because of him. It is not just the love aspects but I feel this spiritual connection to him and know as long as he is safe, so shall I be, or vice versa. It was a miracle beyond human understanding how I have ended up here, but I know he brought me here."

I walked to the window as I watched the drizzling rain start to fall and fog up the land. I told them, "Every night, I see him as he just stands there in the woods and glows like the moon. No one sees him but I so want to see him. I have researched for years into what, how, and why but came up with nothing. Please, I know you are thinking we should just move from here, and so we have been all over the world. He is wherever I am. I don't want to run away but I want to seek the truth."

I told them the night of the bus accident, there was a woman who warned me about my twin flame and her prediction. Her words still ring in my ear.

I told them, "She had said my twin flame was different, very different, and the union between us will rip worlds apart. It shall cross the Earth and beyond as the unknown and known reality will have to open a door for this union. This door is known to all on this Earth as the door of dreams and the door of reincarnation."

Tears rolled down without realizing what has happened to me in these years. I wait for this unknown man every day in my soul. I know it's a mystery, but I still don't know what to do and how to proceed with this.

Grandmother walked over to the kitchen sink as she stared out the window into the park and the lagoon which were watching over us. I love this cottage we have decorated over the last few years. Grandfather had this built for my father and his wife, whom my grandparents never accepted.

Grandfather had a story of his own no one shared but somehow my father never spoke of him as if they never got along. I knew my father wanted my grandfather's approval on everything but never got it. I never asked for I know when the time is right, I will have the whole story.

My grandfather had wood imported from India. The doors, the window frames, and the furniture were all built with this Indian wood. The ranch house looked like a picture book bungalow one would find in India.

So much love they had for my parents, but I guess an elder's ego got to it. He would sit outside with tears as he would repeat, "Why would I the father apologize? Why can't the children just apologize?"

My parents thought they were rejected because of race and religion. It is always arrogance of the human nature that divides. I somehow knew there was more to the story, but my father agonized over this as to why his father had always rejected him, only to let death come over to both without peace being found within either one of them. I only hope the unasked and unanswered questions they had, they have resolved in the afterlife.

As the only living descendant of my family, I want all multi-racial families to cherish life and enjoy the time we all have upon Earth. Right now though, I wanted to unite two zones into one where all humans live and all that is known to the human knowledge. The other zone is the mysterious world where all is unknown.

Nothing is seen or heard, only fear, danger, and yes, love has a pull. How do I find what is unknown and what is hidden? Where do I start from?

Grandmother spoke, as if she heard my mind, "What has been going on might seem strange to you but in this household, it has been like this for centuries. I have never spoken of this to anyone as the mind can be a dangerous place and the wrong person shall hear and spread rumors. You know I am a Catholic but I respect all religions, for who am I to judge? Are we all not the judged? I come from a family of which many were burned through the sixteenth-century witch burnings as accused witches."

She kept looking outside as if she was lost somewhere in the land of memories.

She said, "It may seem strange, but I come from a faraway land where women were healers and called witches. They were burned to ashes for their beliefs. My family was in the practice of foreseeing the future through blessed dreams. As they foresaw their neighbor's obstacles and had tried to intervene or help, they were hung at the gallows or burned at the stakes as accused witches and warlocks."

She held on to her breath as she sipped her herbal tea. She said, "Even taking a sip of herbal tea was like voodoo and magic if it healed a person. So, my family had escaped this curse as they fled the lands of my predecessors as they were burned to ashes for they were thought to be witches."

I thought what was she saying? How and when did this happen? I watched her staring out the windows looking blank. I knew she was searching for her inner strength to go on with what she had to say.

She continued, "I can foresee the future. Through the blessed door of dreams, I get to see my ancestor, who visits us still these days and just disappears like she does not even exist. She was family friends with nuns and seers your grandfather also was related to. I was told in my dreams, your grandfather and I were introduced to one another through this sacred group of people from the past."

I watched my grandmother held her breath and said nothing. Yet we all knew she was grabbing her thoughts.

She then said, "I saw this woman as a child as she had retold the same story you had said but as a child, I had not taken her words to my heart. She had warned me the son I would have will succumb to a sudden death and the child he would have will be different. She would awaken a human through her dreams. Or he, her twin flame, would awaken her for him only. This miraculous union shall be the first holy union given to Earth to show the Lord, the Creator, works from the beyond."

I asked her, "Then why did you not share this with me while we were still in India?"

She answered, "The humans only see what is in front of them and cannot see the beyond. Maybe beyond Earth, the Creator has others like angels who see far more than the humans can, by the will of the Creator. We humans must learn to live with each other and unite and accept the miracles as all is the Lord's will. I can't see what is not shown to me. I only see some things."

My grandmother stopped and she watched me for a while. Then she continued, "I had told all of this to your grandfather as we began our life. He said he would make sure our child does not marry from a different race or religion and all should be okay. Your Aunt Agatha had seen the same visions and dreams as she was warned by her ancestors about this future forecast too, but Agatha decided she would not marry and become a nun so she would escape all of this."

She was deep in her thoughts as then she said, "We all thought we were the ones they were warning us about. When my son Andrew, your father, married your mother Gita, we knew something would come for again she visited all of the family members. You turned to be an adult and nothing happened, so we humans forgot all about this until the accident."

Again I watched my grandmother with all the burden of loss on her shoulders continue to talk as she said, "I know this sounds strange, but I have concluded, why run from what has to be? Why are we scared of this? I know you are brave and can handle this on your own, but I want to be there with you all the way and maybe somehow, I can help and change what was wronged to us. Like it is said, don't be wronged but change what was wronged to you. I assumed India would be a door opener."

I asked, "But Grandmother, what was wronged? What happened that was so wrong, that after all of this time, it is back again?"

She said, "You were wronged by them and so was your love. Both of you were burned because of who you were. I believe you two were separated because of race. We must go and fix what was wronged to you two by uniting the two of you. We can't run from the truth but fight and bring justice to you and him. We must find him, but first step is you must find yourself as you are a human with a gift, not a witch. The gift of seeing the future is in your blood. Find yourself first, then find the others. It's then you shall win at this game that haunts you."

I asked, "How do we do this and who shall help us do this? Where do we start from? Do you say we go out and tell all we are seers and we see the unknown? Also there is a man we see who like travels in his dreams, not teasing or anything, but we are talking about the unknown, the unseen, and the unheard of, where do we start from?"

This time Aunt Agatha spoke. She said, "We start in the Netherlands, as that is where your grandmother, grandfather, and I come from. That is where all this happened, and at least I believe he resides. You were warned to go to the land of the windmills and the land of flowers. It's called the Netherlands, where my forefathers and your grandmother's forefathers are from."

She took a break and just watched outside for a while and said, "Your grandmother's ancestors came from a famous Dutch caretaker named Bertelmeeus van der Berg who had been a member of the Kasteel Vrederic family in Naarden, the Netherlands. He never married yet had found upon his hands his niece, a teenager, who was orphaned when her parents were killed during the famous sixteenth-century witch hunts. The kind owner of Kasteel Vrederic, Jacobus van Vrederic, had rescued the young woman and many other women from the gallows and stakes. He had then taken the responsibility of being their caretaker. Because of that courageous act of a noble Dutchman, we today have your grandmother and you with us."

She continued, "We must find your twin flame first or let him find us. For this mountain to come to us or for us to go to this mountain we have to take some help from a very special dreamer. Yet my only fear is after avoiding the dreamer all of these years, how do I face him now?"

Aunt Agatha, a nun, stood up in the middle of the room and started to whisper a prayer as she started to say, "I live in this time as you live in yours, for let this time call upon you as I call upon you. No religion, no culture, nor race is beyond this as all that is unknown to humans is not wrong for we the humans are weak and call all of this paranormal but oh the Creator of all, let this tunnel be open and let this soul call upon a person whom I had loved before I had given my vows to you. For he had said we were twin flames. I did not marry so how could he? Today I ask if you are truly anything of mine, then come in front of me as I call upon you."

I had thought how were my grandmother and Aunt Agatha related to the seers of the Netherlands. Who was she calling and why did she call him a dreamer? I had no courage to ask.

My grandmother answered as she said, "You said the seer who had come to you said her name was Marinda, right?

Well your grandfather and your Aunt Agatha's family ancestors go back in time to the Netherlands. During the sixteenth century, Aunt Marinda and her twin sister never married but they had a younger sister who did. From them, your grandfather, your Aunt Agatha, and you too are their descendants."

She watched me and then said, "I believe you saw her, because Aunt Marinda does travel time through her mind as she promised to look over Kasteel Vrederic and their descendants even beyond time. Remember the kindhearted caretaker called Bertelmeeus, he and these seers were inhabitants of the same castle during the time period of Jacobus van Vrederic."

She watched me for a while and said, "The dreamer we mentioned, had visited you in India and when it is time you will learn more about him. I believe he will come and pay you a visit when it is time."

I never questioned anything as I knew I was in a family of seers but what more do they have hidden from me? I had no clue. I left the room as I walked back to my own room and realized I missed my parents as for the first time I was scared for what is it that is to come.

As a writer, I can adjust my own place of stay and work but how much more of this unknown history must I take before all of this makes any sense?

Tears are but my best friend as I travel from the land of the unknown through the land of mystery. I wondered what had happened in the past that even in this life, it haunts me.

I wondered about my dream man and smiled to myself as I whispered to him, "For you, I shall fight even my destiny."

I don't know why I kept on hearing the name Jacobus van Vrederic. As if there was a pull toward him, for reasons I could not explain. I missed my twin flame more than I could explain, yet I kept on seeing my little son I had dreamt about in India.

I screamed in my own room hoping no one heard, "Dear beloved, how could I even have a child if I don't even know where you are? Who could I share these secret thoughts of my mind with?"

Then I realized I was in my grandmother's home in Seattle, where I had her throughout the most difficult period of my life. I thought how Seattle became my safe haven even when I felt like I was in Hell. I love Seattle, my home sweet home.

# CHAPTER NINE:

## *Gift Of Love*

*"Love crosses all doors for even time watches over true lovers as they win the battle over even time."*

*Love became victorious as Anadhi Newhouse proved to this world, nothing could keep her separated from her beloved as she crossed even the door of death, only to unite with him.*

I was in bed turning and turning until I went to my dreamland. I was walking with him again, hand in hand as his face came in front of me. His eyes were gray-blue as he stared into my face and asked, "What is it my love? Why are you watching me like you have never seen me in your life? Yet, this twin flame knows your mind, body, and soul only belong to me, as mine are forever yours."

I ran and hugged him as I screamed his name so loud, I wanted all of this universe to know his name. I knew he was my Erasmus, but then I thought his face had changed.

I cried out, "Erasmus," but then I said "Anant!"

He laughed and said, "My love, I love it when you say my name. You know I am Anant."

We held hands and walked as nothing existed but us. I saw we stood at the riverbank where I saw myself and knew I was looking at my own reflection as I saw myself in the water. I knew I was white and had long brown hair and gray-blue eyes yet I was still short. It seemed we became mirror images as now we were both different looking. I was so confused but watched my beloved with a different face.

He was tall and brown, with beautiful brown eyes and raven black hair. He wore an attire like royal knights would wear. I knew from a very young age, we walked and always were together. I would run out with a cloak on as he would escape from his parents' home to be with me. I asked what was it that bothered him.

He watched me for a long time and said, "I don't know but I have seen you in my dreams and I feel like we have been born over and over again only to be separated. I have been having nightmares again and don't want to lose you this time."

He held my hands and as we just sat there for hours, the sun was setting as I realized I must return home before sunset, for during sunset I was not allowed to be out in the dark. I knew I was very different from him, yet he did not care as we held on to each other and saw life just stood still and time meant nothing.

Erasmus's name was different as it was Anant for I called him Anant, yet in my dream I remembered his name was Erasmus. It was then I heard him call my name and realized it too was different.

He said, "Oh no Amara, you must go home and hide before sun down. Put your cloak on and let's run."

I held his hands as we both ran for our life as I knew he was worried for me.

He said, "If possible, I would take your soul and you mine, so I could keep you safe from all this world's unjust forever. Never shall I allow anyone to burn you or hang you even if that would cost my life. Don't tell anyone you see visions and are a seer. I would keep myself lighted for you to find me and unite for eternity. Remember Amara, I only love you and forever this soul belongs only to you."

I cried as I told him, "Please don't leave as every day I find myself awakened in a new time zone, only to see you are not with me. I search everywhere for you yet I can't find you. Please try to find me or give me your given name in this time zone."

My dream shifted as now I was running from a castle and I saw Erasmus as Anant on one side asking me to run and escape as we were both screaming to be together. Somehow, we were separated by a bridge and there were fires burning in the moat below the bridge and all around as somehow, I was to be hung.

I screamed and told all, "I am Anadhi, or Amara, but not Diana the witch. Who is Diana? Why do you all call her a witch? I am not a witch, I have never done anything wrong."

No one heard me as I screamed and I told all, "Leave Erasmus, or Anant alone. He has nothing to do with my family or my kind."

Somehow, I was on deaf ears and no one heard me. I saw the castle light up in glory and all around was smoke and burning of flesh. Nothing scared me as I knew life was nothing. I could escape all of this as I had great powers, that I did not fear death for I knew I was sin free. But I also knew Erasmus would be harmed and I didn't want Erasmus to be harmed or touched because of me.

The night was getting darker as the fire was burning all around. Screams were being heard from all directions. Pain, fear, and death were in the air, but there amongst all were the inhabitants of the cold palace who had ordered all the witch burnings and were oblivious to all of this unjust.

I watched the palace doors open as dinner was being served to the people living inside. Music and laughter were coming from within the castle. I watched Erasmus in this life was Anant and he was being tortured for falling in love with an accused witch.

I watched how bravely he kept on repeating my name and said, "So, let death be gentle, death be kind, even in death Amara, you are still mine."

I saw the moon come up in front of us, a full moon. I knew it was now or never that I pray to the Omnipotent and I said, "Reincarnation is a blessing if only you are mine."

I thought if only he too could remember me in our next life and I prayed, "Let my twin flame be my mirror image. May our souls be connected eternally. For as long as I live, my beloved you too shall live. For as long as you live, I too shall live. I accept you as my husband today, tomorrow, and forever. May my soul always belong to you and your soul always belong to me. I shall always be yours, but with this oath, may my God grant you all the glories of life and let all the sorrows of life be mine."

Everything turned dark as I watched Erasmus, my Anant, my love, my life fade away from my eyes as the sweet smell of death was only mine for my love had the gift from his beloved, the gift of life. I whispered within the air praying this land, this ocean, this air will whisper my eternal love tunes to him throughout time.

I told my eternally beloved, "My love, with all faith await my arrival for not in this life but another, we shall meet. I shall cross the door of death for you. Please remember me and know you have a sacred power within your soul called the power of twin flames. No one can harm you nor death shall touch you unless it is but your will. For even in death, I shall be only yours. Only for love, you too shall cross the door through eternal life. Only for love, I pray my prayers cross the door of life and death and may they be accepted as this is my gift of love."

# CHAPTER TEN:

## *Eternally For You My Love*

*"Eternally yours, twin flames recite as they rise again and again from ashes, yet will destiny be their friend or enemy?"*

*Ferris wheel, the spiritual wagon of reincarnation, was Anadhi Newhouse's last hope, as she tied her lifeline to her twin flame seaching for him life after life.*

I woke up in the middle of the night, frantic and panicking for Erasmus. I placed my hands on my mouth so if I make any sound or cry, Grandmother, Nani, and Aunt Agatha don't wake up frantically. Here I knew my heart just wanted to stop and go back to Erasmus and see him just one more time.

I held on to myself and knew I would give anything to be with him all over again. I know the world still exists and life goes on but I felt my life stopped somewhere in the past. I had nothing but a dream within which I had given my eternal life, my infinite love, and my soul to another soul whom I had no clue about.

How is it even possible to love someone who lives in another time zone, another place, and another land, more than even life itself? Maybe he too was reborn as he said his name was Erasmus. I know memories are blessings in disguise, but does he even remember me?

What if he rejects my love, but then even with the burden of pain, I want to know him. I want to be with him. I want to see him one more time.

I knew the Earth beneath my feet feels missing. All around me, I see pain and these tears just don't stop flowing. I want to scream my lungs out and not stop, for I just want the ocean of tears to get out from this well of mine. This unknown pain just rips my soul out of myself.

Something stopped me on my track as I heard snoring coming from the hallway. Strange, I ran toward the snoring and felt calm and peace as I saw three elderly women sleeping in the open wide room. They kept the door wide open in fear what if I need help.

It seemed as if forever, they had been living like this. Their world came to a stop as I entered their life. My tears stopped in thin air as I knew I love these three women more than my own life. This battle I have inside my body, I must deal with and protect these three women.

These three women are the heartbeats that keep me going and I wanted to live and be alive to protect them. I knew Erasmus is my soul and I wanted to be in the land of the dead with him if he was there. I also knew I must wait for him for what if he too is searching for me in the land of the living?

I put my overcoat scarf on top of my princess pajamas and put my walking shoes on as I went out for a morning walk. Yes, I still wear princess pajamas to bed as that is what my grandmothers, both, gift me. I needed the fresh air and the daylight. I needed to feel him in the glittering morning sun. I wondered if he too was living on this Earth in my time zone.

I thought was the Lord's glorious sun shining over him too? Did he too search for me, or did he have no memories of me? I wondered did he even believe in rebirth or was he different?

I needed the birds flying over to send my messages over to him. I needed to feel Mother Earth beneath me where I fell asleep and he still roamed around, or did he too fall asleep right after me or before me? I was pleading to Mother Earth for the miraculous news, any news she could give me of him.

How do I get in touch with you? How do I call you? How do I see you? Yes, it is true I see something shining in the water at night but it fades as I go near.

How do I find someone who has no address and no phone? Is he human or different? Above all, I don't want the three women whom I love so much to worry about me again now over my emotional pain, after they went through my physical pain.

I looked up into the skies above asking for help, to give me endurance so I can cope with this and may I or may my invisible pain not be a burden on anyone. I was raised a Hindu by my mother so I do believe in reincarnation but was also taught Catholicism by my father. I know there are angels around every corner and they come and show themselves during times of need. I wished for the biggest miracle ever.

A man screamed, "Hey watch out! Do you want to die or something? Woman, are you okay? Hey, if it is a boy you are running away from, let me tell you it's not worth it, for there is always tomorrow! Maybe your boyfriend from yesterday is but a different man today! Find the new and different looking one, don't give up as you bury yourself within the old!"

I saw a well-built African-American man with curly gray hair, around seventy years of age, holding my hand in his as he had held on to me. He looked so familiar as if I knew him from somewhere.

He said, "Hi! James Brown. I live around the corner from your house. I am the preacher in the neighborhood. Your family and I did not get along very well. I guess they don't mind much about preachers. I don't preach religion but to be kind and understanding toward all religions. My main subject is dreams."

I laughed as I felt the warm hand and gave him a huge hug. It seemed like I had known him for ages, for it was James, the dreamer. I felt a mountain of pressure was lifted from my chest.

I told him, "Anadhi. I am from India and I live with my grandmother. I feel as if I have known you for ages. I have seen you in my dream. You are James the dreamer. My grandmother loves company but would never go out and say this. She is actually very soft on the inside, hard on the outside. She is a woman whose nature is of ancient days. You won't find a woman like that in this era."

He laughed and said, "An old soul you are. Seems like you have been traveling time and tide, don't see women like you these days either. I can actually help you, and my dear child it is indeed true, you have seen me in your dreams as I too have seen you in mine."

I asked, "How? What are you saying?"

He smiled and said, "Come on, let's see how kind and warm your grandmother is. I want a warm breakfast with a huge cup of coffee. I want to walk you home. Never married, no children, have been living in this neighborhood for the last forty years. My house is opposite your home on the other side of the lagoon. I see the same view you see every night. Spectacular light show in the water. The moon in her true glory."

I was shocked, what did he say? Does he mean he too sees him my twin flame? I didn't want to think about him, not now in public. I must keep all of this in my mind. Please my Lord, let me be strong like he would want me to be. Yes Erasmus, for you I shall live. For you, only you, I shall give my life.

I walked toward the house as I saw my three favorite women sitting on the porch enjoying their morning coffee. Strange they were not even shocked to see James walking with me. They smiled and were actually happy to see a guest in the house. I knew they too were avoiding the discussion from last night.

Something though was amiss I thought about Grandmother and Aunt Agatha as they were not themselves. I avoided their eyes as I knew I would bubble up at the smallest gesture of kind words from either one of them.

It started to rain and we all walked inside as James broke the silence and introduced himself, "I invited myself in as I wanted to see where this beautiful woman lives. It's a danger, sleepwalking. I really think this woman was sleepwalking, called her from the back, but no answer then we finally introduced ourselves."

Grandmother took over as I left to change and felt better for I needed time to go through all of this in my head. I followed the voices back into the kitchen. The scene in the kitchen shook me up more than I could have imagined.

Grandmother and Aunt Agatha were listening without a word as James talked with authority in his voice, "I would never enter this house in this life or any other, if I could live with this. I can't Agatha. I stayed away from you as that was your wish. You entered the convent and I honored your choice. Never would I have entered any of your lives. I still love you to this day, but I will honor your given oath to the church. She is your niece so I consider her my niece too. My dreams have now brought me back to your home, but I don't come for myself but for your niece, she needs my help."

He stopped himself and then he continued, "Your brother had cut me off and I left at only your words. How could you put her life at risk? She is at risk for she lives with only half a soul. He has the other half. We must find him or she won't make it past her thirtieth birthday and you two know I am the only one who can guide and help them. I am

James, the dreamer, who has walked through the land of dreams. I can help you and take you to him as I too know his name. I will find him with the help of my own dreams."

He helped himself to a cup of fresh brewed coffee and he said, "All of this is a mystery. Some call it an illusion of the Creator. As a seeker, I should know you Catholics don't believe in us, but I stand in front of you as a proof. I do exist and for the sake of love, please can we from all different race, color, and religion, unite and fight to unite the couple as unjust was done to them?"

He sipped his coffee and said, "There is more to life than human knowledge. The Creator who has created humans also created angels, spirits, and those whom you call seers, seekers, and dreamers. Reincarnation is not a fragment of the mind as we all know we had traveled this path as millions of humans across this world believe in reincarnation."

Aunt Agatha stood up and said for the first time, "I believe in the Lord, and even as a nun, I know the Lord creates the Lord's creation. We are just a creation of the Creator. Maybe at the end of time, He wants all of His creation to get along. What worries me is at this time, this stage, people all around the Earth are fighting amongst themselves about religion and race. What would they say if they were told today, there are people who seek the dreamers in an effort to seek the truth following dreams?"

I walked in and without knowing, I broke down into tears. I went and hugged James, rather than my family. I don't know why, but when I looked into his eyes, that's when I saw this kindhearted man who had sacrificed his love for her and yet accepts her wish and is happy. I could not imagine how it must have felt to be all alone and deal with all of this on his own. How strong one must be to handle loving someone so much that you give up everything for your love, and not go crazy or give up on life.

How could any human go through this to lose the love of your life to the church and not go in front of her but save her image and all her love in the heart and still have the heart beating? Why does the heart not give up, like just stop beating? How can you go through each morning and not feel the tears your actions have cost?

Life had stopped for me and I feel this cold feeling as always my inside feels like nothing and all of life seems empty. The sunrise, I want to see with Erasmus. The sunsets, I want to witness with Erasmus. I want to hold his hands and just see him at least once in my life, that he is alive and his heart also beats.

I have spent nights thinking who he is and now I just want to touch his heart and feel the beat, just once please someone help me touch his heart just once. I promise I won't go closer, any closer to him, if that is all of your wish. Just let me see him once even from far away and see him and take a fill of his vision so I can live with this vision forever.

James held on to me as he said, "Sweetheart, all my sacrifice is but not a sacrifice for I hold you today. Remember, soul to soul, remember my child, remember. I give you all the memories of the journeys of past, present, and future."

I could see Erasmus in my head. He was just there crying and screaming as he whispered in my ears not to leave him. Never to forget him.

Erasmus and I recited in union, "Eternal love, soul to soul, from heavens above and Earth beneath, let our love be the spirit of present, past, and future, for within this union, love is complete. For you my love, nothing is a sacrifice. Sacrifice is but not a sacrifice, for within my soul I have my beloved. For eternity, I am but yours."

I repeated, "Dear love, I shall live eternally for you my love."

Then suddenly, I saw I was on a Ferris wheel and somehow Erasmus jumped onto the Ferris wheel. I knew he held on to me as he had a part of my scarf within his hands. He tied one end of the scarf on his wrist and he tied the other end on to my wrist. He said, "Mind to mind, body to body, and soul to soul, for you I live and with you, I shall only die. Know it my love, even in death, I want to only be with you."

I watched the doors of the Ferris wheel had begun to open as I started to fall off. I tried to see where he was but somehow, I saw we got separated and I knew I prayed may we not forget one another. I screamed to awaken Erasmus and I cried for him as I knew he was sleeping. I knew I was falling asleep and only prayed when I am but awakened again, may I only remember you.

I only wondered and recited,

## WILL YOU RECOGNIZE ME?

If I come to you as a bird,
Would you know me?
Would my sweet songs awaken you,
As I only write for you?
If I float above you like a cloud,
Would you know me
As I give you a bath
With my pouring tears?
If I became the moon
Above your home,
Would you know me,
As I light your world
Through my pouring love?
If I became the flower
Growing wild in the garden,
Would you gently pick me up
And take me home?
What if I became

The warm glow of the sun
To protect you from the cold,
Would you open your inner windows
And let me in?
My love, my beloved,
I have changed my form
To be with you,
I only wonder,
Would you accept me
And my new form
Over my old form
That you have painted
In a canvas of me?
I only ask for me,
Would you accept me?
Or for me,
Would you only
Accept my old form?
Dear beloved I ask,
**WILL YOU RECOGNIZE ME?**

I repeated even when I had awakened the next morning, "I shall be reborn over and over again. Infinitely be my destiny for I shall always be yours. These are my vows from beyond, eternally for you my love."

# PART TWO:

# VOWS OF ERASMUS VAN PHILLIP

# PROLOGUE

*"Fallen in love infinitely I had for you and only you, but then how do I see anyone before or behind me as you have sealed my eyes to only you?"*

*Erasmus van Phillip in his study in Scheveningen, the Netherlands, working on his diary.*

R ain drizzled all over my city, as it was again a dark, cold, and very wet day. I love rainy days as they remind me it is all right to let the tears roll for even Mother Nature herself, lets her tears go. Why could a man like me not be allowed to let his tears go? So, today as I watched the rain drizzling outside, I knew I could walk outside without having to hide my tears for only the showers in my apartment in Scheveningen.

Scheveningen, a seaside city beach, which is a district in The Hague, the Netherlands, is my second home. My work place and regular home is in Amsterdam, the Netherlands.

My weekend apartment stands tall in the harbor front resort of Scheveningen. Here I can watch the fishing boats all trying to go out on the North Sea in the very early mornings. I wonder if they too look out for their beloved trying to float back home to them maybe through this vast North Sea.

I am Erasmus van Phillip, a twenty-seven-year-old single European white male, six feet, five inches tall with very pale complexion, brown hair, and gray-blue eyes. This is my sacred diary. The torn pages of my life have found themselves neatly bounded within this sacred diary. Here I can share everything without being judged or criticized by the others. A single man living alone without dating or any interest in dating has so much criticism yet it never bothers me.

For I am a married man, as I had taken the vows of eternally yours to a woman who comes and visits me in my dreams. Hard to believe, but I had held her hands and promised the very beautiful bride of mine, "Forever yours, I am." Night after night, I have traveled to her as she too comes and holds on to my hands.

The pouring rain falling on the sands of Scheveningen beach reminds me of her beautiful, lonely eyes. I know she had told me not to forget her and never to give up searching for her. Yet I don't know how to find her. If I try to even date, I feel my inner mind, body, and soul rip apart into pieces. I sense a lonely wife of mine spreads her tears on top of her lonely pillows all night till dawn.

No my beloved, never shall I let you be hurt or never shall I let you go, for with my memories of you, I shall carry this eternal love story throughout time. Do not fear my beloved, forever I am only yours. For I know, days become nights and nights become days, yet this beloved of yours was, is, and shall forever be only yours. Dear beloved, as long as my heart beats, I am yours and when this heart beats no more, even then, I shall forever be yours. Be my destiny my beloved as these are my vows from the beyond.

# CHAPTER ONE:

## *Left My Soul In Seattle*

*"For you I am as for me you are, so across time and tide, we shall hold on to one another throughout eternity."*

*Erasmus van Phillip saved his twin flame, without even knowing who she was. He knew she was his Seattle Princess.*

"Let my twin flame be my mirror image. May our souls be connected eternally. For as long as I live, my beloved you too shall live. For as long as you live, I too shall live. I accept you as my husband today, tomorrow, and forever. May my soul always belong to you and your soul always belong to me. I shall always be yours, but with this oath, may my God grant you all the glories of life and let all the sorrows of life be mine."

I screamed and shouted and told her, "No, Amara don't leave me. I won't accept anything unless you are mine. I won't accept any life without you. For my love is as pure as yours. Blessed be my love, blessed be our union for that you are mine and I am yours, only yours, from heavens above to Earth beneath, I am yours as you are mine. Let all be witness I give you my mind, body, and soul."

I know I have to come to terms why I keep on seeing dreams where my beloved had died. Tonight again I saw another horrific dream, my beloved was dying and praying for my life to be saved even at the cost of her own life. Over and over, I saw her give up her life for mine.

As the rain poured outside, I thought why I was known as a very stern man who people thought had no compassion. I have bottled up all my feelings for a person whom I don't know if even exists. Also, I don't know why everyone thinks I am very outright and vocal when I have kept everything about myself hidden within the pages of my diary.

Yet today I allowed the tears to wet my pillow. I was tired of wanting someone I barely knew. Life is a dream in itself where some of us play out our dreams in reality, and some wait and walk through their prophetic dreams. After researching through science and religion, I realized dreams are guidance from the beyond. So I told my beloved from the beyond, I would never let go of her or her memories. Like the pages of my diaries are hidden within their covers, my beloved and her memories too shall always be buried within my soul.

As I prayed and prayed, I saw something happened as if Amara was frozen in place and our spirits were holding on to each other. I felt nothing as the Earth and skies above could open and rip me apart for I wanted nothing from heavens above or Earth beneath. I felt all this time I was alive and just now watching my twin flame, my love, disappear in front of me as if she never existed. For her, I didn't want to exist anymore.

The dream was so surreal I did not know what to do. That's when I saw a man appear in front of me as he just stood there and said, "I am James, a seeker. I have been praying to appear and guide you through your dreams. I don't know who you are or where you are but I want you and your beloved to find one another. Your twin flame awaits your arrival. Please believe in your dreams as they are your only guidance."

I realized I was snoozing in and out, so I stood up and wrote my dreams. That was James, the dreamer, whom everyone talks about. He has held a few conventions on dreams and was a preacher I assumed. But why had I seen him?

On a stormy night, he appeared in my dreams as he said, "I travel to unite true twin flames. Remember all come from nothing and all go back to nothing, only thing remaining is memories. Do not forget your dreams for it is in your own dreams she will show herself to you. Yet you, only you must recognize her."

I had met the preacher named James once in Seattle, Washington where he had tried to help and guide me through dreams. He told me all religions were based on dreams so why can't we believe in this mystical tunnel? I told him I will see him in Amsterdam next time he arrives as I had so much to share with him. I never told him about my dream woman and I think I never will.

James, the seeker, a dream psychic, known as a dreamer, who meets and greets people around the globe and talks about dreams also has a rumor to be a time traveler. I only looked him up as I had been visited by him in my dreams. James never talked about his personal life yet is a twin flames expert as he is an expert on dreams.

When I attended his convention, he taught all seekers of twin flames to repeat, "Eternal love, soul to soul, from heavens above and Earth beneath, let our love be the spirit of present, past, and future, for within this union, love is complete. For you my love, nothing is a sacrifice. Sacrifice is but not a sacrifice, for within my soul I have my beloved. For eternity I am but yours."

I repeated in my mind but did not have the courage to repeat it in front of everyone. I never saw him again as after my visit with him, I witnessed a horrible bus accident. A bus traveling with tourists had fallen into the cold waters of the Puget Sound in the Seattle metropolitan area in Washington State. I rushed in and fell in the cold shivering water where I found an Indian Princess drowning. I swear she was as beautiful as a goddess herself but all I could remember is wanting to kiss her and hold her until help came. I don't know if I kissed her, yet I hope I didn't for I never want to betray my eternally beloved.

Yet she held on to me and said, "Anant, never let me go."

I had told her, "I am Erasmus."

She kept on saying, "I know you are Erasmus, but Anant too."

I don't remember what happened, as my Dutch buddies had taken me out of the hospital in Tacoma, Washington. Everyone thought I must have been imagining as no one from the bus survived. Then there was news of a woman who did survive and woke up after being in a coma for a long time. I don't know how I ended up in the hospital. Some people said a taxi driver found me in a church and had left me in the hospital.

I asked around for the woman after I had awakened from the coma, as I too was lying there in the hospital bed in a foreign land for months. My buddies rescued me and I never found out who the woman was. I never had a pull toward any woman in my life as my mind, body, and soul I had given to Amara. Yet why this woman had my mind thinking of my Amara, I don't know.

All I could remember, she was of Indian origin, and it was like she was calling for someone from Indian origin, I think she had said, "Anant."

The name somehow was very familiar, yet I could not remember why, as I don't believe I knew anyone by that name. I only prayed she too finds him. I knew my beloved was European and had brown hair. That's the only thing I can remember of her from my dreams. Over and over I repeated, I only belong to you my beloved, as I am yours throughout eternity. Yet as I had returned to the Netherlands, I kept on having a feeling I had left my soul in Seattle.

# CHAPTER TWO:

## *Recognize Me*

*"Love is felt not seen, then how
would a beloved recognize a
beloved from only his visions, when
they both have risen from ashes
with a new face?"*

*Like the rising phoenix, twin flames Erasmus van
Phillip and Anadhi Newhouse had risen from ashes
through the door of reincarnation yet will they
recognize one another?*

I shrieked and had again awakened from a dream. Each night ever since I came back home, I saw dreams or maybe nightmares. I wondered what had happened back in Seattle that my dream cycle has changed or my memories have increased as I remember much more.

I have kept a diary of my dreams so I never forget or when I finally meet Amara, I could give her my dream diaries. Emotionless man my friends call me, yet how could I tell them I had left all my emotions buried in the past somewhere with a woman I know only as Amara? Yet why Seattle pulls me toward her, I could not explain to myself rationally.

It was a bright sunny morning as I entered Seattle-Tacoma International Airport, from where I had boarded my Delta flight back home to Amsterdam, the Netherlands. The feeling was so strange as I sat on board the plane. I felt I left something of mine back there.

I was hospitalized for saving a woman I did not even get to meet. Yet I felt this amazing connection with her. She was in a coma we had found out, after trying to find her for a while. I eventually got to know she was actually in the same hospital I was in, yet I never got to see her even though I had tried to find out about her after I got well.

The confusion was there were a few accidents involving a few busses that day. One bus had only one survivor. All the other busses had no casualties but a lot of people were wounded and treated at various hospitals.

Maybe one day, I will get to see her, yet throughout the flight back I felt like I was in a whirlwind tunnel of a certain pull. I kept on feeling like my soul kept on telling me, don't leave her. My buddies had told me it was because I almost died in Seattle.

I could not utter my feelings to anyone as only my diary knows my true feelings. The journey back had been emotional as my dreams haunted me more than I thought they would. I had traveled to Seattle hoping to be able to talk with James, the dreamer, yet I only got to meet him briefly as I spent three months in a coma.

Every time I flew, I wondered if I was closer to Amara as I was floating through the clouds. Yet my soul kept on crying as if I left something back in Seattle. From nowhere, tears fell across my cheeks as I kept on asking what pulls me so much. My dreams taunted me even on the flight back.

Scheveningen district in The Hague is my weekend home. An apartment on the sandy beach, near the harbor. Overlooking was the enchanting tall lighthouse.

At night, I would watch this tall structure and think to myself, was she guiding the lost and stranded or just my Amara to me? I asked the night stars to not go to sleep tonight and keep an eye out for my beloved Amara, for I know she is scared but loves the fear-provoking lightning and the piercing thunders of the cold drizzling night. I asked the moon to glow above her house on Earth, wherever she might be.

My beloved, are you too awake thinking about me? My eyes betrayed me as I fell asleep and could not watch the chilling performance of Mother Nature that frightens but also delights my Amara. Again, I watched in front of my eyes, Amara was falling into the deep blue waters and could not come back up.

I knew they killed her. They all thought my Amara was a witch. I knew she could not swim and I screamed and tried telling everyone she was only a dreamer who sees dreams.

There was no sign of her as if the winds, the rain, the Earth, and Heaven had no clue who she was, or where she was. I cried, "Why does it hurt so much? Who are you, that has taken my mind, body, and soul?"

I was tired and sleepy as I said, "No, Amara please don't leave me alone. You must take me with you for this beloved of yours can't continue through the journey of life or death without you. For you my love, I live and for you my love, I shall give my life. How could I forget my own twin flame?"

Then I saw my dream shifted as we were in another time period. All around me was dark, wet, and a very chilly night. The lightning was striking everywhere and all I could see was the sky showing her fury and anger to this universe.

There was a huge castle in front of me, and her inhabitants were celebrating this night as nothing could take away their dinner or peace of mind. Screams of death and fury buried the peace around the castle yet it bothered no one. I realized I was in the time period of unjust witch burnings.

I knew my Amara was sentenced to death because she was accused of being a witch. I tried to rip off this Earth and beyond to prove she was just an innocent human, who was a dreamer. She foretold all of your fate as she saw in her dreams, yet you sentenced her to death even after using her so many times.

I screamed, "Why?"

I just wanted to fall asleep and not feel anything. Mother Earth was flooding all her land as even Heaven above was pouring her tears and fury all over this Earth. Three days and three nights, nonstop rain and fury were flooding everything around the castle.

After all of these curses, the inhabitants of the cold castle were finally worried and thinking of course of themselves. What else would they worry about, other than themselves? This Earth only gave everything possible to them.

Pride and unjust mind of only themselves and their own skin were taunting them. For they all knew, a grave unjust was done. Now all they were worried about was of themselves.

My dream never broke as I watched myself falling asleep on the riverbank, where I had last seen my love. Within my dream, I knew I was asleep, yet I was having another dream. How this was possible I do not know neither could I explain. Yet here I saw my Amara was on a Ferris wheel where I too had jumped on board. I watched we were both on a Ferris wheel where we had our hands tied with a scarf.

She kept on repeating, "My beloved, never let go of our memories, and please recognize me."

I saw her but when I tried to hold on to her, she was not there anymore. She had suddenly disappeared. All that was left of her were my memories and a scarf of hers. I held on to the scarf and screamed my lungs out searching for her.

I watched the skies above and the Earth beneath my feet were just as motionless as they were even when my love was here.

Now as my eyes could not find her anywhere, all things should be ripping apart. The Earth and the skies above should be collapsing in sadness, yet all was as if nothing had changed. I asked the Earth beneath my feet to open and bury me alive. I asked the rivers to take me away and bury me beneath the ocean far away. I asked the mountains to erupt and bury all of this Earth to dust.

Again, I saw I was holding on to the scarf in my hands, the one we both had tied on our hands to never get separated. Yet I only had half of it. Then I, an honorable

Dutchman, repeated, "For you, I was born. For you, I live my life. With you, I shall be reborn for within this union of our mind, body, and soul, we shall unite throughout eternity."

My dream broke and I felt like I had the shivers after a long night of dreams which felt like nightmares. I did not know what to believe as my life only revolved around the given knowledge of this world. Yet how do I find out what is happening if all of this is unknown to the mind, body, and soul? I never believed in reincarnation and made up my mind there must be a scientific reason for all of these happenings.

Yet this long weekend back from Seattle left me in a whirlwind of dreams or maybe nightmares. Again, I saw the same dream repeat over and over ever since I came back from Seattle. The incident that had happened in reality in Seattle, kept on coming back to me like flashes in my dreams. This time a woman was drowning in the cold freezing waters of the Puget Sound. I screamed and asked her to try to swim.

Yet she said, "If I knew how to swim, I would, and I believe every time my life is in danger, you fly over from beneath or above the world to save me."

I tried to awaken her as she laid in my hands like a lifeless body. I checked her pulse and knew she was breathing. I kissed her thinking she was a princess and will awaken with a kiss. She opened her eyes and still was oblivious as she was in a fog or trance or had fainted. I did not know if she could hear me or not yet.

It was then I told her, "Sweetheart, I am from the Netherlands, not heavens above or Earth beneath. I think we are both drowning and that's why I must be confusing you Seattle Princess for someone else as you too are confusing me for someone else."

She uttered very faintly, "I am scared you will find me but won't recognize me. My dying question is my dear prince charming, will you recognize me?"

# CHAPTER THREE:

## *Mysterious Princess*

*"Who are you my mysterious princess that calls upon me in the dark, and holds on to the lantern for me all night, yet at dawn you disappear?"*

*In Varanasi, one of India's most holiest sites, Erasmus van Phillip again saw her yet what kept him from holding on to her forever?*

T he secretive North Sea was wrapped in a numinous cold sea fog. Nothing could be seen except the glowing moon trying to peek through the fog. The Scheveningen harbor had fishing vessels, cargo, and offshore vessels waiting for the fog to lift. There was no maritime traffic today as even the sea wanted all her travelers to take a break.

The tourists walking on the white sandy beach too were missing. I wondered if my weekend home knew tonight I was waiting for a mysterious princess to arrive. If not in real life, then do come and visit me again in my dreams. After the Seattle bus incident, I had to take some time off to alleviate my inner spiritual pain. I needed physical relaxation to get over my physical pain. I did not utter about my good Samaritan act with any members of my family, specially my mother. They only know I was otherwise busy in Seattle.

As a renowned artist, I have my own freedom to work from wherever I choose to work from. I admire the famous Dutch painters Johannes Vermeer, Vincent van Gogh, Rembrandt van Rijn, Pieter Bruegel, and Hieronymus Bosch. It is their given blessings that had placed me onto this path of art and within my canvas, I create my own world. I had painted Amara in different cities, through my eyes.

Strange, I had given her face different ethnicities. Very strange why I did this but I knew I was the artist and my mystical ever beloved had come to life at least on my canvas. I have an art studio in Amsterdam and The Hague. This is why I live in Amsterdam and Scheveningen.

Late at night, my phone rang. I wondered what did people want? Did they not know I like to be left alone in this world, where I live with my blank canvases and my own dream imagination to fill up the canvas with?

I am an introvert and sometimes I feel like I am a loner. I don't like expressing my feelings to anyone, but I am the best friend you can express all your feelings to. I shall be there for all as I am a good listener. I developed this character as I wanted to erase all the pain from the inner souls of the lonely travelers of life. It actually helps me too. I feel good when I know I can help someone from being lonely tonight. Dear mysterious princess, don't worry and please don't be angry as no one could take your place.

After ignoring the phone for a while, I dialed my mother, "Mama, this is Erasmus. Did you try to call me?"

She waited for a while and replied, "No my dear, I did not. You know it was your cousin Matthias as you can see the Caller ID. Also, I don't know why you have not visited me in months. Are you still even in Scheveningen or in Amsterdam? Both my sisters have their sons who have come for the visit, yet my son you are missing."

I listened to her for a while as I knew she was overseas on a trip with her sisters. The three very young women in their late seventies live together after all of them had become widows. My two cousins from two aunts were Matthias van Phillip and Petrus van Phillip who also live in the same household. It's a family home as the three sisters were married to three brothers and had become widows in a very sad bus accident our family tries to forget yet remembers all too well. I had not mentioned my Seattle incident to my mother or aunts for the same reason.

I told her, "I was on a tour with my art as I know you were traveling too. I know you came back this morning by the way. I have kept up on your traveling calendar even though you might think I don't."

She only sighed very loud, meaning she was not satisfied with my answers. She waited for me to say something. Yet we both knew I would only wait, as I never get tired of waiting but we both knew she does.

She said with authority, "I have booked our family vacation for this year for this coming Saturday. Flight leaves at 6 AM Saturday morning. So be ready for a week of traveling. International flight, so do come and join us early."

I knew this was very normal as she had done this every year. I was ready for my notice to join her with my passport and luggage without asking any questions. She gave me complete freedom in living my life my way. So, I always complied with her demands which were very rare but at times very high.

I only told her, "Mama, I am ready and will be there."

She waited silently on the phone as I waited for the words to come and she said, "Erasmus, anything else?"

I told her, "Mama I love you, and always did and always shall, you should know. But I also know it's healthy to express. Yet you know I am not good at expressing."

She waited silently and said, "I know my son, yet I also know you let all of your emotions out late in the night, when you think no one is watching. I am your mother, and I always wash your tear-filled wet pillows. I only wish you could share."

I stayed awake after the phone call for I did miss my mother, but I just could not share my emotions with anyone. So, I kept them well hidden in my inner soul. There was this empty space always in my inner heart where it felt cold and shivering and at times very emotional. All of these feelings were linked to one person. I wish I knew where she was.

Early Saturday morning, I saw my mother at the airport as she even had my passport and visas ready. I found out on the day, we were flying to India for our vacation, instead of skiing in Europe. Luckily, I travel light and knew my mother had my necessary luggage packed with the help of my two cousins.

On the plane, my mother said, "I would like to go to a land which is known as the ocean for spirituality, knowledge, and rejuvenation."

I only kissed my mother's head, which had very prominent blonde and brown hair with gray streaks. Her blue eyes and very stern looks had me on my feet even at this age.

We landed in New Delhi and took another local flight to Varanasi which was about an hour and a half. As we entered the spiritual capital of India, I wondered was there a reason my mother unknowingly brought me here? She always has a hidden reason, neither she shares, nor do I ask.

Varanasi, India is truly majestically beautiful and a very mystical place. It was beyond our expectations. Our tour guide had taken us around the holy city for days as anyone visiting cannot but be amazed by the sight of the Ganges River and all the temples. My two cousins and aunts all had accompanied us as this was a family vacation my mother had planned. My Protestant and Catholic mixed family members enjoyed the very spiritual and Hindu holy sites.

I watched my mother, a Christian woman, walk with the Hindu pilgrims as she respected them and they too were so welcoming and very respectful. I had so many dreams while we stayed in India; however, like usual, I kept my inner feelings to myself and avoided sharing my inner feelings with anyone.

My cousin Matthias said, "I feel like I was here before or maybe it's just listening to everyone, my brain too is confusing itself. How can a person be at a place for the first time yet feel like I have been here?"

I told him, "I don't know, but that's why I have been researching on the topic of reincarnation. I feel like I was reborn over and over again, to only find her. To only search for her and be with her, and I feel like I must unite with her now."

I knew I said it out loud and wished afterward I had not. Yet no one said anything as they only watched me.

My cousin Petrus then said, "Erasmus, we all know you are a sleep talker. You speak about your dreams all night and I think all of your close family members know. We have all tried to give you some space. You know we are not just cousins, but brothers, and your best friends."

I knew they all knew, as aside from sleep talk, my friends who rescued me in Seattle had told my cousins when I was in a coma. As the evening was approaching, the diya lights were gathered on the famous steps of the Dashashwamedh Ghat where people were getting ready for the evening celebrations, and I saw her again. I started to scream as I got up in the crowd and tried to follow my mysterious Seattle Princess.

I screamed, "Seattle Princess! Wait! I need to ask you something. Don't leave without answering who you are. How are we connected? Wait!"

There in between us were so many people doing their rituals, I still ran after the woman dressed in a white and red sari looking like a typical Indian yet I recognized her. She had two women with her who were white Americans. I heard her call one of them Grandmother as she held on to the elderly woman ever so gently. She helped both women and guided them through the crowd. I was trying to follow them as they saw me and watched me for a while. My Seattle Princess linked her eyes directly at me but I felt she was oblivious to her surroundings, like she was in a daze.

I thought the world had frozen as we just saw one another forever. Her beautiful black hair was blowing in the wind. Her eyes were filled with tears as she was praying with her eyes closed. I could not even pray as I watched her and did not want to miss her for even a second. I wished my eyes would not even blink for in fear I would miss her again.

Standing so far away from one another, I tried to catch on to her, yet the diyas floating in the Ganges River and the people performing rituals had kept us apart. I watched her as long as I could and then like a mysterious fog, she disappeared into the crowd. I entered the holy water of the Ganges River and washed my face with the holy water of the Ganges as I tried to hide my tears that could not keep themselves hidden within my eyes.

I wondered why I was trying to catch on to an Indian Princess or maybe the same Seattle Princess, while I saw my twin flame was of European descent. All I knew was this woman and I had a connection, which I could not make out.

My inner soul ripped open for this woman yet I did not even know why.

The last night we spent in India, I had another strange dream. I saw I had been in bed waking up within the embrace of my beloved. In between us was something that had moved. I asked, "Who is it that sleeps in between us?"

I heard a tiny voice say, "Papa, it's only me Jacobus."

Then, he told his mother, "Mama's heart beats my name."

I watched my mysterious princess wife kiss me and she ever-so-lovingly kissed the head of our son.

She held on to him and said, "Forever, my son. Mama's heart beats your name."

I saw our son was white and of European descent. So, my twin flame must be white as I had seen her always. Or was our son like me and she was not European? Is this the reason I am always pulled by this mysterious princess?

# CHAPTER FOUR:

## *The Netherlands*

*"An artist sat by the sea and painted upon a canvas, fields of tulips, windmills, canoes, and colorful cottages. At a glance, you and I know this is the Netherlands."*

*Erasmus van Phillip returned to his ancestral home,
Kasteel Vrederic, with his family and found fresh baked
bread left on the dining table, just like it always had
been throughout centuries, by the castle spirits.*

The Netherlands, a small western European country, is my home. I felt lonely to be back home, as I felt I had left someone behind. We landed in one of the busiest airports in Europe, at Amsterdam Airport Schiphol.

I had accompanied my mother back to her home in Naarden, a city in the Netherlands, in the province of North Holland. It is a twenty minutes' drive from my apartment in Amsterdam. From Scheveningen, it takes me about an hour.

My ancestral home which was built by my forefathers still stands tall. It is a castle, very well known to the locals as Kasteel Vrederic. A flower haven as there are no species of flowers that my forefathers have not planted. The stone castle is wrapped around with climbing wisterias and roses. Carpets of tulips are growing around the property.

A small lighthouse sits on top of the castle which legends say my ancestors traced back to Jacobus van Vrederic's time period. He was known to all as the beloved Opa of Rietje, his granddaughter. The love story of a grandfather and his granddaughter were respected and loved by people near and far.

This lighthouse had mysteriously appeared and was installed, legend says by the parents of Rietje. They are the legendary twin flames of Kasteel Vrederic, who lived and died with one another and were the first ones to be buried at the famous Kasteel Vrederic gravesite, also called Evermore Beloved. My mother inherited Kasteel Vrederic through her family lineage.

The cold castle was converted to a warm family home through eternal love stories created by the van Vrederic family tree. Since my father and his two brothers married three sisters, they chose to live in a multifamily castle as their home. My two cousins and I grew up in this castle.

Kasteel Vrederic is also rumored to be haunted by my ancestors. The only daughter of Jacobus van Vrederic and Margriete van Wijck was known as Griet van Jacobus. Her beloved husband was the famous soldier Theunis Peters.

Griet and Theunis died during the Eighty Years' War. It is said this couple even after their death, were the biggest hand in uniting Jacobus van Vrederic with his beloved wife Margriete van Wijck. To this day, people sometimes do get to see them in the ever-glowing lighthouse on top of the castle.

I entered the elegant dining room of the castle, which opens to the backyard. The walls were framed with huge floor-to-ceiling windows that were remodeled throughout time. Family members, however, always tried to keep the original Kasteel Vrederic and library intact as much as possible keeping the historical monument alive. Also, everyone in the family writes his or her own diaries like I also have kept up, like my ancestor Jacobus van Vrederic, who is still admired by all even on this day. A Dutch nobleman who had always tried to help all whom he could.

On the patio outside, was served breakfast, made Dutch style. There were Dutch apple pancakes and classic poffertjes topped with butter. There on the table was a basket filled with fresh baked bread and freshly churned butter with a jug filled with fresh milk. My mother swears no one bakes the bread but it just appears as needed. I believe, as I had grown up in this castle and have witnessed this rumor as a fact of this home.

My mother came behind me and said, "My son, how does it feel to be home finally?"

I smiled and saw her eager face as if there was some hidden agenda within her heart as she asked me the question. I knew she wanted me to move closer to her, if not back home. My cousins both knew where the questioning was going as they both sat with their breakfast platter.

Matthias said, "Aunt Greta, I know you want Erasmus to move back home. As this castle fell into the hands of the creditors after the family had fallen in hard times, Erasmus bought Kasteel Vrederic back, so we could keep this in the family. It would be nice to see him move back here maybe after he gets married. We will always be here on our vacation or family reunion times. We are blessed we can all enjoy this even though we can't afford this big home or even the cost of its maintenance."

I heard all of them talk and told them, "A family home should always be left in the family unless we can't afford it. I am blessed I can afford to keep it in the family."

My mother was named after her ancestors as Greta, and her sister is Griete, and the youngest sister is Grietje. All three are in their seventies as they are triplets. The three sisters look really similar yet very different, and I could swear I don't know who my mother really is as all of them have raised all of us and to this day, they all claim to be our mothers. Our fathers were very close and were not triplets, yet they died together in a horrific bus accident.

My mother spoke, "So Erasmus, are you dating or do you even have any girlfriends? I know it's hard for you as we all know you are going through some personal dilemmas.

I know you are quiet and don't like to share or I believe talk beyond what you have to. Yet we are all here if you do need to talk."

I started to laugh out loud as that was a trait I had and I could not stop laughing. I loved my mother and knew she could read my mind even if I don't share. I keep my emotions to myself yet I am a crier and a laugher in my own bedroom, and in front of my mother.

She said, "I know you are thinking, why I keep on asking about girlfriends, why you, as you have chosen to walk through this journey of life alone. If you enter the library, you will see all the portraits of the past and the ones you yourself had painted had found their twin flames after a hard journey through life. You should read your ancestors' diaries, then you will see they too had to fight life and death for their twin flames."

I watched her and thought how does she know my inner secrets so well? Could she read my mind?

She said, "No, not yet. I can't read minds but if traveling through India was any rejuvenation of the mind and body, remember the original van Vrederic had fallen in love with an Indian woman. They could not unite and be together. Yet, the son of the union, Jacobus van Vrederic, is the one who had battled against all odds and was victorious to never let go of his beloved."

I watched her and thought but is not my beloved, a European woman? I am so confused as I don't want to ever hurt or be separated from my Amara. I will keep my Amara alive within my inner soul as she is only mine. Forever, my beloved.

My mother said, "I had a dream your wife had come into our home as she told me a story about you and how you had saved her from the cold drowning waters. She did say you could not recognize her as she has changed her face through the door of reincarnation."

She watched me for a while as she knew I would not say anything but only suffer inside.

She continued, "In my dream, I was with my daughter-in-law who I saw was talking with me and I watched Jacobus van Vrederic watching over her. He kissed her head and said as she reminded him of his mother and you of his father, arrogant and suffering inside by yourself, someone must try to get you two united. It was so strange as I watched Jacobus had watched the woman with the eyes of a beloved son."

I walked back and forth at the shock of how Mama would know about the drowning incident. I observed my two cousins who were shaking their heads in denial, in fear I would blame them.

My mother said, "I saw Jacobus walk with an Indian-looking woman who said her name in this life is Anadhi yet it was Amara in her last life. Then, I saw a child jump onto my lap as he called me Grandmother. My dream broke but I hope I can be of help. I know you believe in dreams, so you should also believe in interlinking dreams."

I told my mother, "Everyone in this home had fought with fate and found their twin flames, yet I know Johannes van Vrederic, the original owner of this home, had lost his fight. I am scared to fight with destiny, yet I will keep on trying."

That night, I called my mysterious princess, my twin flame, to arrive in my life. Oh the beholder of my eternal love, my twin flame, may you fly in like the magical bird, the rising phoenix, and fall within my embrace. Life after life, I have waited for you. Never will I get tired of waiting for you my love, even though time leaves me my days to fall into the countdown zone. Sending me a warning sign, time again leaves me to be left all alone, even in this time zone.

My beloved, don't fear for my eternal love shall always grow for you even though my physical body grows old and betrays me every life.

Dear twin flame of mine, if you can hear me then answer my inner calls. For is it not said twin flames can call one another? My love, may my calls awaken you from your deep sleep. May you remember me and like a prayer answered come and arrive in Naarden, the Netherlands.

# CHAPTER FIVE:

## *The Blessed Door Of Dreams*

*"Glowing lights at the end of the tunnels are the blessed door of dreams, that have guided all throughout time."*

*Remembering an elderly Johannes van Vrederic trying to save his daughter-in-law and his granddaughter yet his memories failed him, seen through the reincarnated eyes of Erasmus van Phillip.*

The sixteenth-century Kasteel Vrederic with its everblooming flower bushes feels like a haven. Throughout the years, it fell into the hands of warm and welcoming hearts such as Jacobus van Vrederic. A loved and respected human being and his beloved granddaughter had with their own hands, converted a cold stone castle into a warm and loving home. The cold stone castle, called a manor estate in modern days, found its name from the original owners of the van Vrederic family.

The castle is compared to Johannes van Vrederic who is rumored to have had a cold-stone-like soul. He stayed to himself and not much is known about him except his portrait still hangs in the huge two-story library of this grand home. Along it, are the portraits of Jacobus van Vrederic and his beloved wife Margriete van Wijck, their child, the legendary twin flames who appear in the lighthouse, Griet van Jacobus and her husband Theunis Peters, and their child Margriete "Rietje" Jacobus Peters and her beloved husband Sir Alexander van der Bijl.

All of the family members had lived in this home excluding Griet who was brought back to the castle after her death, in a coffin. Jacobus van Vrederic had even made sure his daughter was brought back home through a war-ravaged country. It is rumored Griet and her husband Theunis still roam around the castle guiding all of the residents of this home.

I wondered if walls could talk and repeat all of the stories buried inside of her, what would Kasteel Vrederic say to us about the coldhearted Johannes van Vrederic, why was he so cold? I was told I looked a lot like Johannes van Vrederic, I sometimes even felt cold and stiff like him too. A trait I do not like or admire. I always wanted to be happy and light like I am floating on air. Except I feel heavy like a huge boulder stone and cold like ice.

That night again, I had a dream. It was so strange as if a church was on fire. I was there and so were so many nuns inside. I ran and found out there was a woman I had known yet as my memories were failing me, I wondered who she was. I was told she was trying to become a nun yet she fell in love with a man and did not know which vows she should keep.

I knew I had some kind of medical problem as I had distress or something and could not comprehend all that was going on around me. I realized I had dissociative amnesia, which accrues from big shock, a trauma, or if one is a victim or even if one has witnessed something horrendous. It made my mind forget things or not remember anything or some things.

And even after the event, I would not recall talking with someone or the events faded. I realized I was in a time period, where they could not relate to the medical terms of the shock. Typically these are temporary, this is why I thought I would be okay for a while yet as if something would happen and trigger it again. I realized the person I saw myself as had this medical condition no one saw or understood. I spoke with the woman in front of me at the moment and hoped I would not forget all of our discussions as I asked her what bothered her.

She said, "I work at Kasteel Vrederic and I don't think the owners very much liked I fell in love with one of the family members. So, I should just take a vow to God and become a nun."

I watched her as she said, "I am married to a person of the castle who might be ruined because of me. I love him more than this world and am afraid to say but I love him even more than life or death and that fears me."

She watched me and said, "So after I have the child, I will give the child back to the van Vrederic family and become a nun. They don't want me and I will never shame them nor never can I live without him. I promised I will never let him go. So, in my heart and soul, I will keep him, ever so beloved, safely."

I told her "Never give up on your beloved, for even God blesses all true love. Take your child and go to him and I know you two can clear up the misunderstanding amongst you two. If you love him more than life, then your vows should only be with him."

I watched her for a while as I was so confused. I told her, "I have memory problems as I miss my beloved so much, I don't know where she is and at times I remember I have a son and at times I feel like I am a lost sailor in the sea. I must go and find her my beloved for they will kill her, or maybe they already have. I am a living dead as I gave all my love to only her. I have no space left in here for anyone. Maybe you all think I am cold and stone hearted but how could I be anything else? For as I lost her, I had to bury all my love and become a stone so I could live without her, for her."

She asked me, "You are confused about who you are, yet you know you have a son. Who is he, and why have you come here to save me?"

That's when I watched myself say, "Jacobus van Vrederic is my son. I am Johannes van Vrederic, the owner of Kasteel Vrederic. My beloved wife was burned in front of me for falling in love with me. They gave me my son and said they would have burned him too but if I could take him far away they would grant his life. I am the cruel husband and father who could not save his wife or give his son a mother. Everyone thinks my wife died at childbirth but I saw them burn her to ashes. Yet I lost my mind because they did not burn me with her. Why?"

I saw I was feeling guilty, Margriete did not get the concept of my mind as my words kept on failing me. I understood the world thought I hated my son because my wife died giving birth, but I guess everyone kept on saying that, as I couldn't protect my own son or his mother or myself as I would get lost in my own mind as I kept on seeing the fires that burned my wife. I forget everything except my wife. I did not know how I could make everyone believe my son is my life as he is the last sign of my eternal love.

I walked for a while as I saw the fire in the church was getting bigger and I told the young woman to run yet I saw she was then giving birth to her child. There was no one to help her as I helped give birth to a member of Kasteel

Vrederic. I tried to tell them this was my granddaughter, I must have her before my memories fail me and I become a stone again. Something happened to me after my beloved was burned to ashes, I lost my memories.

My words became whispers as no one heard me as I tried to tell all I won't remember anything in the morning except I just lost my beloved. I had cursed myself and told all I don't want to remember anything if I can't have my beloved Mahalt. I want to wake up without any memories of anything. Let this world become dark and empty for me, for without you I will be a living dead.

Every time I saw a child was brought over, I would scream, "hide the child" or I knew they will burn it. Don't bring a child dead or alive into my home, they will take it away. Yet I wondered why would some of my words come out and some be like in whispers that no one could hear.

I knew my beloved was burned to ashes as was a church and nuns and a member of my family for I could not comprehend what was going on. I watched a fisherman come in with his wife and I could not hear what was going on as everything became dark. My dark world became darker as I only prayed, "Let even death not touch anyone who is related or has come from my beloved Mahalt. I will cross time and tide for I will be reborn life after life only to find you my beloved, these are my vows from the beyond and I am Johannes van Vrederic."

My nightly screams had awakened everyone in the house. I watched in front of me, my mother, my two aunts, and my two cousins were standing. They all surrounded my bed with their faces leaning over me. Any sane person would be frightened to wake up and find yourself be crowded by a crowd of family members rather than my nightly screams.

I asked all quite calmly, "What is it? Does a man not get any privacy in his own home? As you all are aware, I don't like visitors in my room at any time of the day or night without my permission. Please, I moved out because I love being lonely."

My mother gave me her words as she said, "You can want to be kept alone, but I carried you into this world and for that you are going to be stuck with me. You might like it or not. Those are my rules. I believe I can still have my ways even though you are taller and bigger. I might be smaller than you, Erasmus, still I will be your support now and as long as I am breathing."

The woman has her own way. She could always make me smile, happy, and make me feel guilty at the same time. I watched my very mother still in her pajamas, and told her, "I am all right, just had a bad dream or maybe a nightmare. Yet I needed these dreams to clear out some aspects of my life."

She watched me and said, "You do know you are the reincarnation of Johannes van Vrederic. As that was your first word when you started to talk. We all knew about this, for we have all had interlinking dreams. This house has her own mind and will reveal to all of us what we need to know to tie the loose ends."

I watched my cousins wearing their pajama shorts, carrying their worries all over their faces, as they only watched me and their expression said it all. Either we were all crazy or we were being haunted by a house or I knew I must find her, my beloved. I realized I was being given dreams from my past lives.

Yet, I wondered how many times had I taken birth? I had seen my beloved in different time zones and different forms. I married her in India where she was burned, then I had seen her be burned down as a witch, then I had seen her drown. How many times did I awaken in life to only unite with you my mystery princess, and when will I find you?

I knew I must not waste another lifetime as we were separated life after life, but in this life I have the blessed gifts of the spirits of Kasteel Vrederic for they have blessed me with my memories back from the past, through the blessed door of dreams.

# CHAPTER SIX:

## Do You Believe?

*"I wait for you burning my candles,
I walk behind you only to support
you, yet when will you but believe
in me?"*

*From the shadow, twin flames Erasmus van Phillip and Anadhi Newhouse appeared in front of the Lover's Lighthouse of Kasteel Vrederic, pulled by the spirits of the castle.*

The full moon glowed behind Kasteel Vrederic tonight. I stood in front of the lighthouse installed by my ancestors or so as I believe my own son, my daughter-in-law, my granddaughter, my grandson-in-law, and my great-granddaughter. All the family members who through their prayers have brought me back again to this home. I watched the home and knew why the circle of life had brought me back here once again. I must do what I had refused to do throughout time and never give up but take a vow like all of my family members.

So I said, "I shall never let you go, my mysterious princess."

I promise not just to my beloved but all of my family members and non-family members, if you too fall in love, I will be there for you, as our home will be there for all twin flames eternally throughout time. I felt strange as I have seen dreams all my life to be guided back to my twin flame. Yet, I believe tonight I was guided back through my dreams to my own family home.

I believe in you Griet, as I know you have been burning the lantern for me to return to our home. I believe you are the granddaughter whom I, like a fool, had turned away from our home. I know you were waiting for me to return home, as even today you stand behind me to bring back all my memories through your lantern of hope, your blessed lighthouse. Did you know I had painted portraits of you and your twin flame, the great soldier of our family, from my mind as I saw your grandmother in you, through my eyes, yet in this life through the door of dreams?

I ask you and your husband, the great soldier, to guide this form of me as I am just Erasmus, an artist, who is in love with a woman from his dreams yet I don't know who she is. I know she was Indian in one life, yet I saw her as European in another. I only hope I know her and don't make a mistake.

I watched a male and female figure appear in the lighthouse in front of me. My cousins were out keeping an eye on me. Even though they wanted to be invisible, they were very visible. Everyone in the courtyard saw the lantern glow up ever so brightly and there in front of all, was a loving couple holding on to one another.

I realized I saw our ancestors, Griet and Theunis in an eternal embrace as they were in life and in death. I wondered how I had seen them as they only appear when true twin flames are standing next to one another. At least, this is the famous legend our home Kasteel Vrederic is known for.

That is when I heard voices behind me. There was a group of people entering our home over the historical bridge that was here from the sixteenth century. A woman with a very faint voice was talking with my mother.

She said in American English, "Hey, everyone did you see? The lantern above your home just glowed so bright! There were two ghostly figures standing on top of the roof, waving to us. I thought they were kissing. Oh my, I never knew ghosts too kiss."

I wondered how she saw the spirits of Kasteel Vrederic when not everyone could see them. I thought the legend said you must be next to your twin flame and one of you must ask and if it is true, the spirits appear. I wanted to be alone and just ignore my mother's friends. She has friends from around the globe visiting the historical castle regularly.

My mother interrupted when she said, "James, my dear friend, I can't believe you truly accepted my invitation. It was my dream to meet you at least once in my lifetime. I am your biggest fan."

James had with him a lot of people. I wondered where have they all come from? I watched the lighthouse flicker in front of us. That's when I saw the woman who spoke without thinking speak again.

This time she said, "Oh my, it seems someone here is thinking rude things. That's why the spirits of Kasteel Vrederic are upset. Watch they have their hands folded across their chest in an angry form. I wonder who could be upsetting even spirits."

The moonlight glowed all over the courtyard as I could barely see the stranger with sharp and honest thoughts. I saw James, the dreamer, as I wanted to tell him I had so tried to connect with him but the bus accident had taken me off of my path.

James watched me and said, "Nice to meet you again, Erasmus. I am blessed to be able to bring with me my four favorite women in this world. We travel in search of destiny. We have come across our belief for we must walk to destiny if destiny does not come to us."

I told him, "The honor is all mine as this household could have some guests, some brave people who are not afraid of bumping into the spirits of the past. For the rumors are, this castle is haunted. But all the spirits are very friendly so there is nothing to be scared of. We were all actually praying to be able to meet up with you at least once."

James said, "My friend Sister Agatha's niece is like my own niece, and she is a huge fan of yours. She has purchased a lot of your artwork, and really wanted to ask you about one of your portraits. That's how she got in touch with your mother and it turns out your mother is her biggest fan. As my niece Anadhi is the author of so many books, one book specifically talks about her dreams."

I watched my mother hug a small petite woman. She said, "I have been praying for this miracle and I can't believe you really came. I see today the full moon is shining above our home yet today I know a moon goddess is standing in front of me in our courtyard. You know what, I feel like Jacobus van Vrederic, the famous diarist, our ancestor, would have loved to welcome you himself. For him, I do it today."

I felt like I was missing somewhere in my own selfish land where I wanted some time with my own self. I wanted to be left alone to figure out what I should do to bring destiny to myself. I did not want any visitors but I knew I had to talk with James selfishly. For the first time in my life, I felt really guilty to ask for a favor without being of help and doing something without expecting anything in return.

I saw the small petite author talk again as I realized she must be an extrovert or very innocent and can't keep anything in her mind.

She said, "You read my book *Dream Diaries* as it's just my dream diaries. I believe in dreams and I feel like they call upon us and guide us throughout our life. I was not sure about this trip but in my dream, I saw I was standing in front of the lighthouse of Kasteel Vrederic so I am here with the people who too believe in all of our dreams."

She watched the lighthouse and said, "The dream to be here was given to all of my family members, my two grandmothers, my grandaunt, my friend James, and myself. No one questioned when you called on us to be here. We believed it was a sign, maybe given to us by the spirits of Kasteel Vrederic through the divine powers."

She watched me directly and asked me, "Do you believe in dreams? I wanted to ask why on Earth would you make a portrait of me as one of your biggest artworks to this day? Did we ever meet? Somehow, I feel like I know you but how? How could you have drawn all the details of my face without ever meeting me?"

She kept on asking as everyone watched me carefully. I saw her face in the moon's glow. I thought she really was a moon goddess and she was standing in my courtyard.

All I could hear was her question, "Do you believe?"

# CHAPTER SEVEN:

## *Will You Be My Shadow?*

*"A lonely soul walking alone, fearing loneliness, asks its own soul to seek its twin flame and become one another's shadow."*

*Erasmus van Phillip and Anadhi Newhouse bumped into one another, spilling flour all over their faces which again prevented them from seeing one another.*

K asteel Vrederic was in a jovial atmosphere. The smell of fresh baked bread spread throughout Kasteel Vrederic. The household members were busy as if finally we too were having Christmas in July. The castle had all of her windows and doors open to welcome the pouring sunlight, as if she too was rejuvenating the inner home. I wondered who had opened all the windows and doors to welcome the morning sunlight. I knew my family members kept the heavy draperies on as if they kept everything safely inside and all the unwelcome outer world outside.

I found the culprit as I bumped into a very petite elderly Indian woman. She was breezing through the home and singing in Hindi, while she was busy with my mother cleaning and cooking. I wondered how a guest I barely knew felt so warm and welcoming. I actually wanted her to be around more. She gave me the feeling of happiness. That's when I saw there were two other elderly woman of European descent who too were busy cleaning the huge castle.

I knew my mother was a brutally honest and an outright truthful person, who because of her attitude could not have any friends. But it seemed somehow the overnight guests became her buddies. I realized the guests must be really friendly and welcoming that they even converted my mother into a very good-humored and content mood. I watched out for a certain person who was nowhere in sight. I don't know if I got upset she was not here, or because I did not like my inquisitive mind. Why did she pull me toward her, as if there was a connection?

I must keep my distance and not be bothered by her, for neither was she my Seattle Princess nor my Amara. I needed to take a break from all of these people, so I thought maybe I would make some excuse and go to Amsterdam for a few days. I did want to talk with James but he had already left for a convention. He will be back to pick up the women who were invited by my mother.

My mother is a huge fan of the dream book author. Maybe we can all gain some much-needed help or even a little knowledge from her. As I was thinking about the author, I bumped into something very soft and warm and somehow electrifying to the touch of my very inner senses. She had a huge bowl of flour in her hands as she and her flour bowl fell on top of me. We both fell backward somehow and she landed on top of me.

She immediately said, "Apologize now as you hurt me. My heart could have stopped beating you know. I thought I broke the expensive flour bowl. I believe it is your family heirloom. I could have used a cheaper bowl to mix the dough for the roti, but I enjoyed using this one. I felt rich and like I was living in eras gone by, like a Renaissance woman."

I could not control myself but started to laugh so loud. She almost cried out and said, "You are rude like people say the Dutch are. Do you know over the years, how many times I have defended the Dutch people, only because I believe my twin flame was born from this blessed land?"

I saw she was covered in flour and still lying on top of me. I never told her to get up because it felt amazingly good to have her on top of me. Then I remembered a face of the woman whom I searched everywhere for and then I helped this very petite woman up.

I told her, "It was my fault as I had not seen you. You should wipe your face and I can help you to the washroom where you can help yourself wash off the flour. I would also love to show you some artwork of mine in the library as you had accused me of painting your face. I have yet to see your face for last night it was too dark, and now you are covered in flour. I too would like to see the face I had painted without my knowledge."

She watched me for a while and said, "Actually I had wanted to sue you for painting my face without my permission. But Uncle James had told me there are always more answers to our questions. He told me to look into the perspective of the perceiver, maybe there was another reason. Also, I have never sued anyone and don't find peace in the idea. It's just that everyone keeps on asking how much I was paid to be a rich and famous painter's model. I, however, told everyone I don't charge anyone to take my picture. It's all my pleasure. You can keep a portrait of me even if you can't have me."

I burst out into a laughing fit at her answers or questions. Controlling my outburst, I told her, "That's ridiculous as the painting was done recreating old portraits of my ancestors. If you would allow me, I will show you after you clean up. I shall also go and clean up. Also, if you are anything like my ancestors then you would be like a person I met in Seattle."

We both left in different directions as I did not know what to say to a person who is so brutally honest and kind and somehow I am again pulled toward her. I had then found her wandering around Kasteel Vrederic. She had changed and was wearing a blue hand-embroidered dress which had forget-me-nots on it. I knew my ancestors were all very fond of forget-me-nots. I told her nothing as she was facing backward.

She was bent over and looking up backward as she was a very petite woman, inspecting a portrait hung very high on the wall. This was a portrait of Griet van Jacobus, one of the ancestors of this castle, and the famous known spirit of this home. I wondered why she was so into the picture. She was shaking and I felt so bad that I held her from the back. She shivered for a while even in my arms as I wanted to see her face but said nothing. I wondered about my Seattle Princess, whom I was so attracted to, and knew it was because she reminded me of not Griet, but her grandmother who was so similar yet somehow different.

She asked me, "Who is this woman and when was the original portrait from?"

I told her, "The granddaughter of Johannes van Vrederic and the daughter of the beloved diarist Jacobus van Vrederic. The portrait was from 1590, and I believe it was her wedding portrait. The person next to her is her husband, the great soldier who had rescued my family honor. From this couple, our family has continued even to this day."

Then she said, "Why does she look Indian, if your family is of European descent?"

I did not answer for a while but then told her, "Because Johannes van Vrederic had fallen head over heels in love with a woman of Indian origin and had brought their child back home with him. It just so happens Johannes had died but his granddaughter looked just like her grandmother. We don't have any official portraits of her but I have it on very reliable sources, Johannes's wife looked just like Griet van Jacobus. My sources had told me, Mahalt, the wife of Johannes van Vrederic, had a black dot on her cheek. So on my copy portrait of Griet, I have placed a black dot to recreate the wife of Johannes van Vrederic."

That's when for the first time, my guest turned and faced me. In shock, I stood silent for so long, as in front of me was standing not Griet but Mahalt. It was then, I also realized this was my Seattle Princess, for which reason I was so pulled to her, because she resembled my Mahalt. The model of my painting I had done, was standing in front of me.

I watched her as she said, "If there are no pictures of Johannes van Vrederic's wife, then how did you come up with a black dot like mine, on the copy portrait you had created of this woman?"

I told her, "I don't know the answer but I had created the portrait at a very young age as I had seen her in my dreams years ago before I saw you even in Seattle or I believe in India. I want you to tell me, how do you have a black dot on your cheek that Johannes van Vrederic's wife had, yet no one has a picture of, except my portrait? How did you get it, answer me?"

I thought to myself I made no sense. What was I saying? This woman was getting the better of me.

She jumped at me and said, "I must have stolen it from your dreams of me and pasted it on my cheek so you would recognize me. Remember my poem? I had asked you, will you recognize me?"

She stopped herself in between as she only watched me and said in a whisper, "You too are a dreamer? So you wanted to meet up with Uncle James because you are a dreamer."

She had tears roll out of her eyes and roll onto her cheeks. I wanted to wipe off her tears. Yet I did not place my hands on her cheeks because I did not want any attachments with a person whom I did not know or could not connect myself to or did not want to connect myself to in fear of what if she was not mine. Then I thought, what if she is mine, just mine, and my twin flame? Was she reborn over and over just for me? I asked my heart to guide me as to why I felt the entire existence of my being was standing in front of me.

She then asked, "May I see the portrait of the father of Griet, the diarist, Jacobus van Vrederic?"

I told her, "Yes, this way, this is him right here, next to his beloved Margriete, his wife."

I watched Anadhi walk over to the portrait. She asked me, "May I be permitted to touch this portrait?"

I told her, "Yes, you may. They have been preserved."

I watched her touch the painting and cry slowly. I wondered why she was crying like she saw a child of hers for the first time or something. She hugged herself so tightly as a mother would do after she realized her child was no more. She watched me for a while.

She then said, "He does look a lot like you, and I wonder since you don't have any portraits of his mother, do you have any portraits of Johannes van Vrederic?"

I told her, "Yes, right over on the next wall, all by himself as he was a loner and not a happy person. I am told I look a lot like him."

She walked over very slowly, touched the portrait, and said a phrase in a whisper so I could not hear but I heard her.

She said, "Yes, Erasmus, you too look like yourself, is it not strange? I was yours and shall always be yours, even if you don't remember it matters not as I do remember. I only ask this Kasteel Vrederic and the spirits of a favor. Please help me and if you can't be mine in this life too, at least I ask you, will you be my shadow?"

# CHAPTER EIGHT:

## *Prophesied At Dawn*

*"A dreamer's dreams become prophecies only when they are seen by all at dawn."*

*Jacobus van Vrederic brought Erasmus van Phillip and Anadhi Newhouse together in front of one another even from beyond his grave, for he knew his mother as she too knew him her son, in any form or time.*

T he night came as she gifted us with inexplicable bright star-filled skies. I realized how I got immersed into the famous painting *Starry Night* by the world-renowned Dutch painter Vincent van Gogh. I could watch the stars all night and not let any thoughts enter my mind.

Yet this night, I kept on wondering where a certain talkative, very direct guest had disappeared to. My talkative princess was ever so quiet all day. The night at Kasteel Vrederic came too soon.

All day I missed her. I knew she was rolling out her tears for the unexplainable emotion of love for people she never knew yet knew all too well. Everyone in the household too knew she was upset and made excuses for her.

I must stop wondering about her for she is just another stranger whom fate has made me encounter for a few days. Temporary guests come and go, leaving us with memories we can't detach ourselves from. She never asked me about how I had saved her in Seattle. She never even asked how I saw her in India.

Maybe she just doesn't care. Yet who is she? My mind wondered why were we thrown together over and over again and why does my heart beat only for her?

I told myself whoever she is, I will avoid her contact and let it go, as I must find my Amara. If she was mine, she would have said something, about remembering me too. What if she is married happily ever after?

Just the thought of her being married to another person ripped my inner guts out. I felt like I would rather die than have to encounter that fact. But why am I even letting this woman take my mind, body, and soul and rip them apart? Anyway, she did not have a ring on.

I cried my heart out as I told my twin flame Amara to appear for I miss her too much. I don't like missing someone so much whom I don't even know. I know I was Johannes, as my entire family had interlinking dreams aside from my own memories.

Yet I wonder why this unknown woman was crying over Jacobus, my son from my past life. Weird it may sound, but I know he was mine and so are all the van Vrederic family members. Yet why did she almost break down at his portrait? Was she really his mother?

I heard sounds late into the night but I knew everyone in the house was fast asleep, or I thought them to be at least. So, I followed the sound. I ended up near the library where the ancestral portraits were displayed.

I heard voices come out as I heard Anadhi say, "I don't know why it hurts like I just lost my son. The same child that said, 'Mama we have to go to Seattle and then to the Netherlands.' The dream I had in India is displayed on this wall. I know it's weird but that's my son whom I never got to hold. I have to go back home without telling Erasmus I am his Amara. But how do I leave my heartbeats back in the Netherlands when I must keep living? Does a person not need her heartbeats to survive? But Erasmus is my Anant, my Johannes, my twin flame. He is my heartbeat."

Then I heard another voice say, "Listen to your grandaunt. You must tell him, or have James tell him as he too is trying to find out who he is. Remember if you have seen all the dreams, then it is very likely he too has seen."

Then Anadhi said, "As a dreamer, I know the basic rules. We cannot awaken a sleepy dreamer for it could damage him forever. He is my heartbeat. I can't harm him even in my death. I will just go home without ever letting him know the gray-blue eyed, fair-skinned woman he is searching for has changed and now is an olive-skinned Indian woman with black hair and brown eyes."

I heard her whimpers and knew my heart ached to be with her, yet how do I accept her as I always saw my twin flame to be European? What have I done? Why does my heart too cry for her? Why is it my mind, body, and soul say she is mine and I shall never let her go? Yet why does my physical mind ask how could all of these be true? I never believed in reincarnation or twin flames until I was born with memories of my past.

I made a vow to my twin flame as I told her in my mind, "If only you are mine, I shall never let you go, Seattle Princess."

I stood outside the library where Jacobus van Vrederic had written his *I Shall Never Let You Go* diaries. It is the same library where Rietje too had written her *I Shall Never Let You Go* diary. This library had converted all of its beholders to create a diary called, *I Shall Never Let You Go*. So, you my author, should know I too shall never let you go if you are mine for within this same library, I too have written my *Vows From The Beyond*.

I let her family be with her as I stood and waited outside for her to calm down. My mother came downstairs and I saw my two aunts were with her. The three sisters were all very different looking as they were fraternal triplets. Yet they were identical in their love giving and sharing.

My mother handed me a book written and published years ago by my Seattle Princess. My mother said, "I know you have already decided to reject her as you allow the scientific reasoning of your mind to decide for you. Yet I only want you to read this book as it has your dreams written inside of the blessed pages. The book was published years before you had told anyone about your dreams or before I too had shared with anyone my own dreams."

I held the book in my hand and thought how long was this in our home and why no one gave me this book before.

My two cousins came downstairs and watched me as my mother said, "They brought the book back with them, from a book convention. We never told you as we followed the author's advice and did not want to awaken a sleepy dreamer. Yet I had my worries so I did get in touch with James, the dreamer, and asked for his help. Now go read the book and you do as you wish but please don't delay your decision and live to regret yet another life."

Everyone left as I watched Anadhi walk to her room quietly and stop in front of my room. If only she could see I was sitting in the parlor where I could see her from yet she could not see me in the ever so dark room. By God, I know who you are sweetheart, as even when everything fails, my heartbeats know. For they have even in this life, only belonged to you. Dear Seattle Princess, my heart beats only your name.

I asked her mind to mind, "I am in the parlor, would you join me, for is it true twin flames can talk mind to mind?"

She turned around and walked back to the parlor. She searched for something as she spotted me in the dark. She watched me for a while as we allowed the darkness to evolve around us and not say anything to one another. Yet somehow I knew this woman would not give up without saying anything.

The woman who can't keep anything in her mind would not just walk away without even trying. No, I knew the person my heartbeats belonged to would fight until the last breath. I, too, sweetheart will try and fight for you until my last breath.

She sat in the parlor next to me in the dark. She said, "To be noticed, you must be in the light. For if you hide in the dark, no one will notice you, nor will anyone say anything in fear of getting buried in the dark. If you call upon your twin flame like the nightingales calling one another, you must at least learn to sing like them."

I watched her and told her, "Yet I love the dark night for within the ever so darkness, I can hide myself and no one would bother me. Yet it is so rewarding to see my candles of hope glowing even in the dark. For I know she keeps the candles glowing for her lost lover to find himself back home to her."

She told me, "If you want the answers, you must knock, seek, and ask. You can't wait for them to be dropped off on your lap. If you want to be kissed, you must show yourself and see the person you are so wanting to kiss. Remember Johannes, you kept all of your feelings buried yet it is your son who has unburied them even after being buried himself."

I asked her, "Why would you call me by that name?"

She said, "Because you lost everything in that name and must get out of the dark to find everything in the light holding on to that name as support. Dreams are guidance from the beyond yet one must be guided to understand their own dreams. For the messages are given not at once but throughout time."

I watched her for a long time as I told her, "Twin flames and reincarnation were not instilled within the societal beliefs, so I questioned myself. Why should I accept these? What if I am wrong? What if I fall because I took the wrong path?"

I saw she did not even get angry as she watched me and said, "Twin flames know one another as they rise from the ashes like the rising phoenix and call upon one another. Through dreams, I have found my twin flame and I know who he is and where he is, yet I will never let him know about myself. I want him to wake up on his own way and own term. For if he comes with his own realization, then he is mine. Yet if he does not, then he never was."

I watched my brave warrior as I knew who she was. I read her book alone all night as I saw she fell asleep crying in the library. I realized a mother had lost her son and just found out the truth. I did not want to take away time from a mother and her son. So, I let her be with Jacobus van Vrederic.

Somehow I knew all the spirits of Kasteel Vrederic were watching over us. I only hoped I too can watch over a very strong and brave woman in this life and pray it's not too late. In the reflecting pond outside, I could see the lighthouse above our home.

It seemed like dawn was about to break open, when I saw in the lighthouse there were more than two people watching over us. I asked my son to guide his mother back to me and help me, a father, who has so much to say yet can't for the life of me say a single word. I wished I was not an introvert and could just say my words.

She said, "A dreamer's dreams are prophesied as dawn approaches and we don't need the help of a candle to guide us anymore. We must realize the truth at dawn and not waste the whole day yet again to be cloaked by yet another dark night."

I watched her and told her, "It's dawn, Seattle Princess, will you give me your hands and be my life support? For I really don't want another day to be wasted and be engulfed within another dark night. I had awakened over and over again with a different face, different name, and at times in different places, only to seek, knock, and ask for your hand in marriage."

She stood up and said, "If only you are mine, I shall never let you go. But dear prince of my dreams, be a nobleman like your son and ask me properly. Forever I have cried and asked the skies above and the Earth beneath, if he is mine, he will arrive. I have said if I am yours, you will know. I have said if we are twin flames, you would never forget me but remember everything we had shared and be mine eternally. I always believed you would know me through all the physical changes for how could you not know when I know who you are?"

I watched my brave princess and told her, "Lost and stranded I was through the memory lanes of the reincarnation route. Yet through the miracle door of dreams, I have found myself first and so then I found you my beloved. For it is true we are born in two bodies yet are one as you are mine and I am your twin flame. Our eternal love story was blessed and proven through our interlinking dreams seen by more than one set of eyes in the dark nights yet today as I ask you to be mine eternally, this love story would be prophesied at dawn."

# CHAPTER NINE:

## *Spirits Of Kasteel Vrederic*

*"Heavenly bells ring and the blessed candles glow as they too call upon twin flames to unite throughout time."*

*Anadhi Newhouse and Erasmus van Phillip finally got to see their spirit son Jacobus van Vrederic from centuries ago, through the door of miracles, called the eternal love of a mother and father which never dies, not even in death.*

awn finally broke through with the sun's blessed glimmers of hope pouring in through the open doors and windows of Kasteel Vrederic. The nighttime musical team of singing birds continued through the night as they handed the session over to the daytime musicians. The nightingales finally took their break, and the robins and thrushes started to sing their part, as they then turned it over to the blue birds and sparrows. I wanted to join them and sing to my beloved and let her know my heart's inner kept secrets. Throughout time, I have stored all my memories of her and the grief I had stored for her, with only her.

This morning, I knew James, the dreamer, was coming back and had wanted to take the four women he had chaperoned to the Netherlands back home to Seattle. The women had all toured the Netherlands as sightseers, except one individual never left the house. I never knew why she wanted to linger on in the house but realized it was the mother in her soul. She wanted to hold on to the son she never knew or held yet somehow was connected through an amazing door of dreams.

I watched the glamorous beautiful princess of mine elegantly walk all over Kasteel Vrederic as she was forever tied in a knot to this home. I wanted to talk with her and get to know all of her inner heart's desires, regrets, sorrows, and joys. I wondered does she not even realize how much I miss her, even though I knew she was only sleeping like a princess only a few rooms apart from me? Early dawn, she had walked very elegantly back to her own room and stayed there.

I felt a warm breeze behind me as I knew she was there. Never do I ever have to see, hear, or feel her, for I just knew it was her. Without any notice, she came behind me and hugged me so tightly I was shocked. I turned around and kissed her right on her lips. She did not object but responded right back. Forever I had only wanted to feel like this. My heartbeats raced fast and knew it was because I finally had her within my embrace.

I told her, "Mystical princess is not shy, as I thought you might be."

She watched me and said, "No, it's all in the movies. They wait forever. I had waited forever for you, life after life. I realized waiting only made me lose you. Every time you only disappeared like a fog. My dreams end and you are no more. I go to bed alone and wake up alone, yet in the middle of the night you come and visit me and leave me with so much love and only memories of the past and tears of separation."

I watched her and knew exactly what she meant. I held her within my embrace. If only I could keep her in my embrace throughout eternity. I wondered how easily she speaks of my mind and my feelings, yet knew they were her feelings too.

I told her, "You are mine as I have crossed life after life to only unite with you, my sweetheart, my mystical princess. Never shall I let you go, this is my vow. I had promised you, I would cross life and death only to be with you, and today I have found you. Evermore beloved, eternally, never shall I let you go."

She asked me, "I saw you in Seattle, how?"

I thought for a while as we walked to a place I wanted to show. Without questions, my Seattle Princess walked with me, hand in hand. Not far from the main house, we had a coach house that was converted to a guest house through the years. Yet, there near by the coach house, was my family burial site, we call this the *Evermore Beloved* garden of forget-me-nots. Beautiful blue forget-me-nots grow here as do all different shades of flowers one could imagine. A swing was made by Jacobus van Vrederic and his beloved granddaughter Rietje that still swings on a huge tree that withstood the years even though humans have left this Earth.

Anadhi walked past me to a gravesite so beautiful. She sat on the bench that was resting beside it. The bench said, "Opa's heart beats Rietje forever. Opa lives on eternally within me and all the residents of Kasteel Vrederic infinitely."

I told Anadhi, "This is the gravesite of Jacobus van Vrederic, the famous diarist, and his beloved wife Margriete van Wijck. This bench was created by their granddaughter, everyone calls her Rietje as her diary reads. Yet she called herself, 'Opa's heartbeat.' She too became a famous diarist as her love story is also famously recorded and found through her words in her personal diary. She, however, wrote her famous phrase as she had from a very young age said, 'Opa's heart beats Rietje.' It is said she also had a hard time explaining to herself how could she marry and share her heartbeat as it was given to her Opa. She explains this detail in her diary, *Entranced Beloved*."

Anadhi only walked and saw all the van Vrederic family graves as some had different surnames through marriages. Yet all whom wanted to be buried here had been brought here as per their wishes.

She said, "It's strange to see all of this and tell anyone that I know who these people are. They are my babies. If only I could have held on to my granddaughter Griet and tell her this Oma's heart beats her name. All of you should know I have crossed the door of death to only say, my heart beats all of your names. Forever you are all mine through the door of eternal love. Forever we are all tied through immortal love, even though life is mortal."

I watched the woman who shared all of my inner feelings and thoughts. How could a person on this day stand and feel the emotions of a mother or a father or a grandfather or a grandmother? Only I would know as does my twin flame.

I told her as she sat next to Jacobus like a mother watching over her son, "I was in Seattle trying to get in touch with James. I was by fate sent to the area of the bus accident. I don't recall much but I jumped into the Puget Sound as I watched the bus dive into the deep, cold freezing water. I found you and thought it was all a dream as I had awakened in the hospital three months later."

She cried and asked, "How could you risk your life?"

I laughed and told her, "Sweetheart, I never risked my life as I saved my life. For don't you know, I had to be there as the beholder of my life was at risk?"

She held on to me and asked, "What about India, why were you in India?"

Again I told her, "It's my mother as she too is a dreamer and somehow knew you would be there. She is related to Jacobus van Vrederic and I believe somehow she knows what she has to do. The difference between the others and her is she has courageous determination that normally people would not have. In this instance, she is more like her namesake, Griet van Jacobus, the woman whom everyone watches to appear in the lighthouse alongside her husband Theunis Peters. Legend has it, it was her body that was brought back to the castle after her father Jacobus van Vrederic finally located her. Dead or alive, he wanted his child back home."

I watched the beautiful garden as I told her, "Legends say, the grandfather Johannes van Vrederic was cruel and did not allow his granddaughter to enter. Yet, my memories say it was different as I believe it was my past life. I had lost my wife in a brutal and mean way and had lost my mind."

I watched Anadhi for a while and saw she just waited for me to finish. So I continued, "I remember living in a trance or a fog as my mind could not comprehend anything happening around me. I would walk back into the painful world where my beloved wife was burned in the fire for falling in love with a white man."

I stopped as she held on to me and said, "Do continue Erasmus, as I too need to know what had happened after our romantic endeavors. All I remember is there was a rich merchant who had come to India and swept me up off my feet. Night and day, I would secretly meet my beloved. We even married in a typical Hindu tradition. I was so much in love with my beloved. Yet, then I only remember I was being burned alive and my son was taken away from me. Everyone told me he would never come back. They talked about my husband."

I told her, "I did go back. I actually never left as they held me prisoner and I only was able to leave with our son Jacobus van Vrederic somehow. I don't know what happened as I must have done a good job. He did turn out to be a nobleman. Yet I had trouble remembering anything as I only wanted to be with you."

Anadhi held on to me in a hug as she said, "I had seen I was born as a white European woman at one point and you were Indian. Somehow I was not able to hold on to you as I tied your hand with mine."

I told her, "Then, there was another life where you were burned as suspected of being a witch."

I watched her as she watched me for a long time and we both placed our heads onto one another for a long time.

She said, "Promise me, we won't allow anything to separate us, not religion, not race or color or beliefs, for it's hard crossing over life after life alone and in fear. I don't want to do it alone anymore. Remember you are my Johannes as I am your Mahalt. You are my Anant as I am your Amara. And in this life, I am Anadhi and you are my Erasmus."

I watched her and thought how strange it was, that this woman in front of me had installed within her chest all of my secrets yet I never had to tell her anything. Everything was like a dream, however in the daylight, I saw my dream princess, my twin flame, and realized my dreams have come true.

I told her, "Beloved twin flame, I have risen only to unite with you, evermore be mine and never let go of me as I shall never let you go."

That's when we both saw in front of us were standing the spirits of Kasteel Vrederic. We both saw our family members were all there in front of us.

For the first time, I saw my son Jacobus van Vrederic who said, "Welcome back home, Mama Papa. Let this life be a blessed journey together, in union forever."

We both found out we had so much in common as one more thing was, we were both criers. Tears were our best friends. But these were happy tears as we both knew our inner most secrets, we were both dreamers.

Back at Kasteel Vrederic, the family members were all planning our wedding ceremony. The Seattle trip was canceled as the only event that was being planned was the wedding ceremony. We had all agreed we wanted our marriage ceremony to be at Kasteel Vrederic. We did not have to tell everyone we wanted all the members of Kasteel Vrederic to participate, the seen and unseen guests. Lights flickered as the lighthouse lantern glowed letting everyone know, tonight a prayer had been answered.

James, the dreamer, had finally entered our home. We had lit the castle with candles and lanterns. Tonight we had all wanted a small wedding ceremony that one would only find in the sixteenth century to take place.

This wedding should have taken place in the sixteenth century. Time was our enemy yet faith was our friend and through fate and belief, we finally had again tied the knot in the twenty-first century. Watching over us were all the past, present, and just maybe the future members of Kasteel Vrederic. It was then, everyone attending the wedding saw cheering from above were the spirits of Kasteel Vrederic.

# CHAPTER TEN:

## *Conclusion Chapter: Dreamers Throughout The Ages*

*"Dreams continue throughout the ages even though the dreamers do change."*

*Jacobus van Vrederic was reborn again to his parents to only unite them from beyond and be their son once again. His last wish was granted, "Be my destiny, vows from the beyond."*

*D*awn found her ways back at Kasteel Vrederic as all the inhabitants knew this home would always have fresh baked breads for all who enter. All the people searching for true love would also find their twin flames if only the enchanted mystical lighthouse lantern glows approvingly.

This dawn, the castle finally had closed the chapter to a story that had begun in the sixteenth-century Netherlands. The story like a river, a sea, and an ocean had continued to travel through time and land as it went all the way to the land of mystery known to all as India and landed near the Ganges River. The story also took its turn and landed near Seattle at the shore of the Puget Sound. Then the story finally turned its course and ended at the shores of the North Sea as it finally found its happily ever after. Three countries, three continents, were tied in union through a sacred love story.

My diary has recorded this charming, magical, and mystical romance story throughout time. Who says life is only a journal where the stories are written and forgotten throughout time? Who says love stories end at death? Here in this home, we believe love stories never end for true lovers will travel time and tide to unite with one another. Twin flames will rise like the magical phoenix, from ashes only to unite with one another.

If you happen to forget your beloved as you suddenly find yourself awakened in another time zone or another land, then become the singing birds of the nights and call upon one another. Ask the night stars to guide you through the night. Ask the singing birds to awaken your twin flame. Do ask the bright moon to glow and be there as a lantern throughout your sacred journey. If you still can't find your way out of the dark, then come to Kasteel Vrederic and stay here for a while. Maybe you too will be guided back upon your path.

In my home, Kasteel Vrederic, we believe in true love stories and eternally ever after. For within the walls of this home, are buried only true love stories that shall inspire twin flames to rise and call upon one another. We don't fear death nor do we fear life for the only thing we fear is being left alone.

Today I have come to the conclusion chapter of my diary as I have included my beloved wife's private diary within my diary. This was our combined choice as we decided our love story belongs in one diary not two, for you all know, in union we the two became one. Twin flames are complete individuals individually, yet when united they become one. Our words are sacred gifts from our inner soul to this one world of love and lovers. I would want all of you to pick some inspiration from our union and spread love throughout your life. Through these pages, create a path to your destiny.

Believe in destiny yet know it is you who controls your destiny as you are never destined. For when you take the steps, you control your end destination. If lost like in one life or another, remember to get back on the road and take the exit to get back on track and find your own destiny.

If only misunderstandings could be erased within one lifetime, we would not have had so many broken families. I never had a grudge or never hated any child as my own son misunderstood me. I never wanted any couples to be separated, yet blinded by my own grief, I was not even in control of my own mind.

I was scared of anyone else falling in love and losing his or her beloved. I wanted to keep all couples happily married forever in my Kasteel Vrederic. I wish I could go back in time and repair the damage. Yet I believe my honorable son did repair the damage I had committed without knowing.

My wish was honored by all the inhabitants of Kasteel Vrederic and so twin flames are never separated yet find one another as they enter or pray in front of our lighthouse. My wife today sleeps next to me as we have again started our life together. A life we thought could never be yet is because we believed.

My second wish was also granted as I wanted my son to know I loved him more than life and wanted to hold him and let him know one more time. Shrieking cries broke the amazing morning when I realized the sounds were of a very young child. Today I have him again in my life.

For today I watched with astonishment, love, honor, and pride, our honorable two-year-old son come and walk into our room. I was shocked at how amazingly he looks like a certain someone I had known and loved beyond what words could describe. He was named after the great diarist Jacobus van Vrederic whom he resembles. We call him, Jacobus Vrederic van Phillip.

Anadhi jumped up and held on to our son as her motherly nature asked him, "What is it my child? What bothers you?"

The crying child walked into our bedroom crying and having a fit but he usually was a very happy and fun child.

He said, "Mama, I saw a dream. It was scary! I had walked in a flying taxi with you and went to Seattle and then finally found our home."

Anadhi knew as I did too, what he had said for we too had foreseen his birth dream. But we looked at one another and thought what was he talking about? Were there some stories missing in his stories too?

We both looked at one another and said, "Oh no, here we go again."

Jacobus watched us and said, "Mama's heart beats Jacobus."

I watched a mother and a son who were separated life after life, finally unite. I told both of them, "My heart beats my whole family, all of you here and all of you not here but were and shall always be my complete heartbeat."

I told my mystical princess, "Sweetheart, my answer to your question from your diary was, is, and shall always be yes, I will recognize you. You had written your beloved poem as you had asked, 'Will You Recognize Me?' My answer is in a poem only for my beloved."

## ANYWHERE, ANYTIME

My sweetheart,
If you were a bird, I would be
Your singing nightingale.
My beloved,
Your sweet songs are
My singing grace I awaken with.
My love,
I will take a shower
Within your pouring tears
As your eyes store my tears.
My dear,
How could I not know you
As you are my only world
Made out of my love.
My soul,
If you become the moon,

I shall be your everlasting glow
For we are always one.
My life,
Within my chest,
Your everblooming
Wild flowers grow.
Forever your home
Is but my inner chest.
My evermore,
I have kept my inner windows
Closed for the world
As only you reside within
And glow from within.
My darling,
If you become the river,
I would become an ocean
To accept you.

If you become the heartbeat,
I would become the heart.
If you become the stars,
I would become the night
To unite with you eternally.
My twin flame,
Eternally I shall be yours
Through life and beyond death.
Through love and for my love,
I shall always call upon you
And shall recognize your calls.
*ANYWHERE, ANYTIME.*

My answers got me a sweet passionate kiss from my beloved wife. We kissed one another as our son "Jacobus" watched over us. We renewed our vows each morning with a kiss and a promise. We said in union, "Reincarnation is a blessing if only you are mine. In every life, be my destiny, vows from the beyond."

*To all of you readers, these two diaries are here signed by,*

*Erasmus van Phillip*

and

*Anadhi Newhouse van Phillip*

P.S. Don't forget to walk back in time to the seventeenth century and read *Entranced Beloved: I Shall Never Let You Go*, where you will find out how my ancestors Margriete "Rietje" Jacobus Peters and her twin flame Sir Alexander van der Bijl united. Through the union of Rietje and Alexander, today in the twenty-first century, we still have Kasteel Vrederic and our dynasty continues. Yet before you revisit Rietje's diary, you must stop over and visit my son, Antonius van Phillip and read his diary *Heart Beats Your Name: Vows From The Beyond* first. How do we know about our future dynasty, you might ask? It's simple as in this house we are all dreamers. We see the future and the past. Keep reading our family diaries and you too shall know. Also, do remember within this home, we had and shall always have as our gifts for all of you, dreamers throughout the ages.

My Dear Readers,


This novel is the third book in my *Kasteel Vrederic* series. Within this book, you can see how everything in Kasteel Vrederic had begun and where the inhabitants of Kasteel Vrederic are now on this day. Next you will find the fourth book in this series, *Heart Beats Your Name*. Then I will take you back in time to find out what had happened to Rietje and her beloved in the fifth book in this series, *Entranced Beloved*. I hope you all give this family your love and blessings.


-Ann Marie Ruby

# THE INHABITANTS OF
# BE MY DESTINY

**Anadhi Newhouse**  Author, daughter of Dr. Andrew Newhouse and Dr. Gita Shankar Newhouse, granddaughter of Martin Newhouse and Miranda Newhouse, and granddaughter of Hari Shankar and Parvati Shankar

**Erasmus van Phillip**  World-renowned painter, twenty-first-century owner of Kasteel Vrederic, son of Greta van Phillip, and descendant of the van Vrederic family

**Miranda Newhouse "Grandmother"**  Seeker, paternal grandmother of Anadhi Newhouse, mother of Dr. Andrew Newhouse, wife of Martin Newhouse, and descendant of Bertelmeeus van der Berg from the *I Shall Never Let You Go* diaries

**Martin Newhouse "Grandfather"**  Paternal grandfather of Anadhi Newhouse, father of Dr. Andrew Newhouse, husband of Miranda Newhouse, brother of Sister Agatha Newhouse, and descendant of the family of Aunt Marinda from the *I Shall Never Let You Go* diaries

**Hari Shankar "Nana"** Maternal grandfather of Anadhi Newhouse, father of Dr. Gita Shankar Newhouse, and husband of Parvati Shankar

**Parvati Shankar "Nani"** Maternal grandmother of Anadhi Newhouse, mother of Dr. Gita Shankar Newhouse, and wife of Hari Shankar

**Sister Agatha Newhouse "Aunt Agatha"** Nurse and nun, paternal aunt of Dr. Andrew Newhouse, grandaunt of Anadhi Newhouse, sister of Martin Newhouse, and descendant of the family of Aunt Marinda from the *I Shall Never Let You Go* diaries

**James Brown "Uncle James"** Dreamer, seeker, dream psychic, and preacher

**Greta van Phillip "Mama"** Mother of Erasmus van Phillip and descendant of van Vrederic family

**Griete van Phillip** Aunt of Erasmus van Phillip

**Grietje van Phillip** Aunt of Erasmus van Phillip

**Matthias van Phillip** Cousin of Erasmus van Phillip

**Petrus van Phillip** Cousin of Erasmus van Phillip

| | |
|---|---|
| **Dr. Andrew Newhouse "Father"** | Father of Anadhi Newhouse, son of Martin Newhouse and Miranda Newhouse, husband of Dr. Gita Shankar Newhouse, descendant of the family of Aunt Marinda, and descendant of Bertelmeeus van der Berg from the *I Shall Never Let You Go* diaries |
| **Dr. Gita Shankar Newhouse "Mother"** | Mother of Anadhi Newhouse, daughter of Hari Shankar and Parvati Shankar, and wife of Dr. Andrew Newhouse |
| **Jacobus Vrederic van Phillip** | Son of Erasmus van Phillip and Anadhi Newhouse |
| **Dr. Jonathan Zhang** | Intensive Care Unit physician |
| **Rian Ahmed** | Tour guide in India |
| **Aunt Marinda** | Sixteenth and seventeenth-century inhabitant, and spiritual seer from the *I Shall Never Let You Go* diaries |
| **Jacobus van Vrederic** | Sixteenth and seventeenth-century owner of Kasteel Vrederic, Protestant preacher, son of Johannes van Vrederic and Mahalt, husband of Margriete van Wijck, father of Griet van Jacobus, grandfather of Margriete "Rietje" Jacobus Peters, and the |

diarist of the *I Shall Never Let You Go* diaries

**Margriete van Wijck**   Sixteenth and seventeenth-century inhabitant, beloved wife of Jacobus van Vrederic, mother of Griet van Jacobus, and grandmother of Margriete "Rietje" Jacobus Peters from the *I Shall Never Let You Go* diaries

**Theunis Peters**   Sixteenth-century inhabitant, honorable soldier, husband of Griet van Jacobus, father of Margriete "Rietje" Jacobus Peters, and son-in-law of Jacobus van Vrederic and Margriete van Wijck from the *I Shall Never Let You Go* diaries

**Griet van Jacobus**   Sixteenth-century inhabitant, daughter of Jacobus van Vrederic and Margriete van Wijck, wife of Theunis Peters, and mother of Margriete "Rietje" Jacobus Peters from the *I Shall Never Let You Go* diaries

**Margriete "Rietje" Jacobus Peters**   Sixteenth and seventeenth-century inhabitant, seventeenth-century owner of Kasteel Vrederic, granddaughter of Jacobus van Vrederic and Margriete van Wijck, daughter of Theunis Peters and Griet van Jacobus, wife of Sir Alexander van der Bijl, and inheritor and co-

diarist of the fifth diary in the
*Kasteel Vrederic* series

**Sir Alexander van der Bijl**  Sixteenth and seventeenth-century inhabitant, great-grandnephew of Sir Krijn van der Bijl and husband of Margriete "Rietje" Jacobus Peters from the *I Shall Never Let You Go* diaries

**Bertelmeeus van der Berg**  Sixteenth and seventeenth-century inhabitant, caretaker of Kasteel Vrederic, and non-blood related uncle of Jacobus van Vrederic from the *I Shall Never Let You Go* diaries

**Johannes van Vrederic**  Sixteenth-century inhabitant, original owner of Kasteel Vrederic, husband of Mahalt, and father of Jacobus van Vrederic, from the *I Shall Never Let You Go* diaries

**Mahalt**  Sixteenth-century inhabitant, wife of Johannes van Vrederic, and mother of Jacobus van Vrederic

**Anant**  Previous incarnation of Erasmus van Phillip

**Amara**  Previous incarnation of Anadhi Newhouse

# GLOSSARY

Get acquainted with some Dutch and Hindi words, places in the Netherlands, India, and the United States, and historical or religious figures and terms that were used in this book.

| | |
|---|---|
| **Act Of Contrition** | Christian prayer for forgiveness |
| **Agra** | City in Indian state of Uttar Pradesh, home of the Taj Mahal |
| **Amsterdam** | Capital city of the Netherlands |
| **Amsterdam Airport Schiphol** | One of the busiest airports in the world and main international airport in the Netherlands |
| **Ayodhya** | One of seven holy pilgrimage sites in Hinduism, in Indian state of Uttar Pradesh |
| **Banaras** | Another name for Varanasi, one of seven holy pilgrimage sites in Hinduism, in Indian state of Uttar Pradesh |
| **Bengal** | Region that spreads across two nations, India and Bangladesh |
| **Bremerton** | City in Washington State, in the US, on the Puget Sound |

**Buddha** — Philosopher and religious figure known as the founder of Buddhism

**Catholicism** — Christian faith that follows the Roman Catholic Church led by the Pope

**Chambers Bay** — Golf course in University Place in Washington State, in the US, on the Puget Sound

**Chief Si'ahl** — Native American chief of the Suquamish and Duwamish tribes for whom the city of Seattle is named, also known as Chief Seattle

**Dashashwamedh Ghat** — Stairs that lead into the Ganges River, near the Vishwanath Temple in Varanasi, India

**Dhyana** — Meditation, term first used in Hindu scriptures in the Upanishads

**Diya** — Oil lamp made of brass or clay

**Dutch** — Term refers to both the language spoken and the people in the Netherlands

**Dutch apple pancakes** — A type of pancake with apple slices

**Dwarka** One of seven holy pilgrimage sites in Hinduism, in Indian state of Gujarat

**Everett** City in Washington State in the US, on the Puget Sound

**Ganga Aarti** Prayer to the Ganges River

**Ganges** Natively known as Ganga, a sacred river in Hinduism which flows from the Himalayas into the Bay of Bengal, and is worshipped as the Goddess Ganga

**Goddess Kali Temple** A temple dedicated to the Goddess Kali in Hinduism

**Hail Mary** Prayer in Catholicism based on Biblical scripture praising and requesting Mother Mary's intercession

**Har Har Gange** Hail Mother Goddess Ganga

**Haridwar** One of seven holy pilgrimage sites in Hinduism, in Indian state of Uttarakhand

**Himalayas** Mountain range that extends across a part of Asia including the border between India and Nepal, highest point is Mount Everest

**Hindi** Language spoken in India, one of the official languages of the Indian government

**Hindu** A person who practices Hinduism

**Hinduism** Oldest religion and third-largest religion on Earth according to scholars

**Holy Rosary** Prayers recited by Catholics on rosary beads including Hail Mary and Our Father

**India** Officially the Republic of India, country located in South Asia, and the second most populated country in the world

**Indira Gandhi International Airport** One of the busiest airports in the world, located in India

**Indus** River that flows across Asia from Tibet into the Arabian Sea

**Islam** Abrahamic religion, second-largest religion on Earth according to scholars

**Janmashtami** Hindu festival celebrating Lord Krishna's birth

**Jonathan Edward Back** Seattle cabinetmaker

**Kanchipuram** One of seven holy pilgrimage sites in Hinduism, in Indian state of Tamil Nadu

**Kasteel Vrederic** Castle Vrederic is the home of the van Vrederic family in the *Kasteel Vrederic* series, spanning from the sixteenth century through the present

**Lakewood** City in Washington State in the US

**Lord Hanuman Temple** Temple dedicated to Lord Hanuman in Hinduism

**Lord Krishna** Worshipped in Hinduism as the supreme God

**Lord Shiva** Part of Hindu trinity consisting of Lord Brahma as the creator, Lord Vishnu as the preserver, and Lord Shiva as the destroyer.

**Lord Shiva Temple** Temple dedicated to Lord Shiva in Hinduism

**Mahāmrityunjaya Mantra** Great Death-Conquering Mantra recited to the Three-Eyed God, Lord Shiva, appeared in the Hindu text *Rigveda* of the Vedas

**Mathura** One of seven holy pilgrimage sites in Hinduism, in Indian state of Uttar Pradesh, known

as the birthplace of Lord
Krishna

**Muslim**   A person who practices Islam

**Naarden**   City in the province of North
Holland in the Netherlands

**Nana**   Maternal grandfather in Hindi

**Nani**   Maternal grandmother in Hindi

**New Delhi**   Capital of India

**North Holland**   Province in the Netherlands

**North Sea**   Sea off the Atlantic Ocean,
expands across different
countries including the
Netherlands

**Olympia**   Capital city of Washington
State in the US, on the Puget
Sound

**Oma**   Grandmother in Dutch

**Opa**   Grandfather in Dutch

**Our Father**   Also known as the Lord's
Prayer in Christianity, a prayer
taught by Jesus Christ within
the Bible

**Pacific Ocean**   Largest ocean between the
continents of North and South
America and the continents of
Asia and Australia, also borders

Washington State in the US on the western coast

**Pike Place Market** Market of different businesses including Farmers Market in Seattle, Washington in the US, created in 1907

**Poffertjes** Dutch mini pancakes

**Port Townsend** City in Washington State in the US, on the Puget Sound

**Puget Sound** Body of water off the Salish Sea and the Pacific Ocean within Washington State in the US

**Roti** Type of flatbread popular in Indian subcontinent

**Sapta Puri** Seven cities in India known as seven holy pilgrimage sites in Hinduism including Ayodhya, Mathura, Haridwar, Varanasi, Kanchipuram, Dwarka, and Ujjain

**Scheveningen** Seaside resort and fishing port on the North Sea in The Hague, the Netherlands

**Seattle** Largest city in Washington State, one of largest seaports in the US, on the Puget Sound

| | |
|---|---|
| **Seattle-Tacoma International Airport** | One of the busiest airports in the world, main airport located in Washington State |
| **Sutta** | Buddhist scripture |
| **Tacoma** | Third-largest city in Washington State, one of the largest seaports in the US, on the Puget Sound |
| **Taj Mahal** | UNESCO World Heritage Site located in Agra, India |
| **The Hague** | Political capital of the Netherlands within the province of South Holland |
| **The Holy Spirit** | Part of the Holy Trinity in Christianity along with God the Father and God the Son |
| **Thornewood Castle** | Estate located in Lakewood, Washington in the US |
| **Ujjain** | One of seven holy pilgrimage sites in Hinduism, in Indian state of Madhya Pradesh |
| **University Place** | City in Washington State in the US, on the Puget Sound, home of Chambers Bay |
| **Varanasi** | One of seven holy pilgrimage sites in Hinduism, in Indian state of Uttar Pradesh |

**Vedas**   Religious scripture in Hinduism

**Washington State**   Northwest state in the US
bordered by the Pacific Ocean
on the west

# MESSAGE FROM THE AUTHOR

*"Love withstands time. Time leaves us as she crosses our door. Love leaves us with sweet and sour memories, as she crosses even time. For even when all but ends, love survives through eternal vows."*

Dear Readers,

I hope you all have enjoyed your visit at the magical Kasteel Vrederic and the van Vrederic family. Don't forget to wish as you leave Kasteel Vrederic and the inhabitants of this home. By the way, you never know who is listening, and just maybe the spirits of the Kasteel Vrederic might overhear and grant your wishes. Never give up on true love for it's the only miracle that will always come true, if you only believe.

If you forgot to wish, don't worry as this book is your forever free pass to visit Kasteel Vrederic whenever you want or as many times as your heart desires. Don't forget to collect all the other books in this series to enjoy the complete magical visit.

This series had taken me on a magical mystery ride where I wondered what would happen if the stories through life could have been rewritten. I thought if mistakes we had committed could have been omitted, but then I realized life is a one-way path where there is no return entry but just exit. The answers we don't find in life always bothered me.

I wondered if there was a parallel world where we could see what was going on in the sixteenth century and again in the twenty-first century. It's not possible as the bridge of life is only a one-way path unless, however, I could be the writer. So, in this book, you the reader can take a trip down the memory lane and back as within this book you too could be traveling with the characters back and forth. This is the third romance fiction book in the *Kasteel Vrederic* series.

Infinite love is the eternal truth this universe revolves around. So, I have hidden a sacred message within the twin flames of this eternal endless love story. Their names carry a hidden infinite message from the beyond. Anadhi-Erasmus and Anant-Amara, both pairs in union, mean infinite love. Again, the names Johannes-Mahalt in union mean infinite love from the grace of God. As I wrote in this eternal love story, I have brought to life twin flames who don't give up on one another in life or in death.

While writing *Eternal Truth: The Tunnel Of Life*, I learned and now believe life does not end at death. Dreams have been my complete guidance from the beyond. Blessed I am to have this gift as I call myself a Dream Psychic. Within this timeless book, I have taken the miracle door of dreams to again answer my inner question of what if the door of dreams could unite twin flames. I believe this is possible through the door of faith and belief. Allowing the door of dreams to guide, you could actually complete your destiny or be at the destination, if only you believe.

To make my "what if" dreams unite true lovers, I have now written this passionate romance, based on the "what if dreams could become a reality." Here, I use the blessed door of dreams to bring to you another infinite endless romance novel. This romance novel crosses time and tide allowing the door of dreams to be the guide. Love is eternal. Love lives on beyond time and tide. In this book, I have brought to life, eternal love, for even death could not come in between true twin flames.

What is death? It's the end of this Earthly body, this vehicle the Lord has blessed us with. Yet have I not proven to you in my book *Eternal Truth: The Tunnel Of Light*, death is nothing but a tunnel we enter to either reenter Earth or be with our Lord? If twin flames are destined to unite, they shall, but only if they both accept their destination as one another.

The spirit, the soul, lives beyond the grave as scientists throughout time have proven dreams are not fictional but the complete truth. All major religions on Earth too were based on this miracle door of dreams. Now through this proven path, my characters too have conquered love throughout time.

Forever love is immortal, as are twin flames, for they call each other from far beyond time and tide. They have the Lord's blessings called the miracle door of dreams. Did you ever think what if dreams can unite true lovers? Dreams have more depth in them as dreams have been a path to prophecy throughout time. Through dreams, twin flames have also united in the pages of this book.

A diary of one's written yet not bound pages goes unnoticed and sometimes lost through the windstorms of life. Yet the bound pages of a book will enter your home if only you accept. We watch waves go by yet, never come back. My characters have crossed land, water, and the skies. They have crossed over eternity for is it not said, true love conquers all, even death?

Based upon prophetic dreams, you will see how twin flames have united in this book. The plot is based upon my faith in dreams. As a dream psychic and a believer in prophetic dreams, I have written this book to fit the world of romance using the world of dreams. This book is fictional, yet the door of dreams is real. I have again placed pen to paper to awaken you to the world of what if, as I believe you should never give up on your twin flame. It is your love, your belief, and your eternal truth.

For even if life is blocked off through boulders called destiny, I could then through the pages of my book, give another couple a chance or let them call upon one another through belief. What if they could only call upon one another and say, "If only you were mine"? What if they could say, "Be my destiny even though you are not mine yet"?

They will call upon one another like the nightingales of the night. They will rise like the rising phoenix and say, "Forever my twin flame, I am forever yours. These are my vows from the beyond." So, today through the pages of this book, I bring to you another endless and timeless love story where it matters not what happens in the end but let the love story be written. You don't fall in love choosing the end, but the eternal, infinite, and immortal love story you the beloved write through your footprints.

The landscape in this book is based upon my personal travel journey, yet again written as to fit the storyline. All characters and storylines retell a forever treasured and eternal love story. The countries and cities, however, are real and here within the pages of my book have become alive, through my eyes and my pen and paper.

Don't leave this book without hope and belief in true love. Remember twin flames and their eternal love stories have made history in the past. They are creating stories today in the present. Forever eternally they shall rise like the phoenix from the ashes to only unite with one another throughout time. My message to my beloved readers shall always be, faith is believing not questioning.

# ABOUT THE AUTHOR

Ann Marie Ruby is an international number-one bestselling author. She has been a spiritual friend through her books. The bond between her readers and herself has been created through her books. The blessed readers around the globe have made Ann Marie's books bestsellers internationally. She has become from your love, an international number-one bestselling author.

If this world would have allowed, she would have distributed all of her books to you with her own hands as a gift and a message from a friend. She has taken pen to paper to spread peace throughout this Earth. Her sacred soul has found peace within herself as she says, "May I through my words bring peace and solace within your soul."

As many of you know, Ann Marie is also a dream psychic and a humanitarian. As a dream psychic, she has correctly predicted personal and global events. Some of these events have come true in front of us in the year 2020. She has also seen events from the past. You can read more about her journey as a dream psychic in *Spiritual Lighthouse: The Dream Diaries Of Ann Marie Ruby* which many readers have said is "the best spiritual book" they have read. As a humanitarian, she has taken pen to paper to end hate crimes within *The World Hate Crisis: Through The Eyes Of A Dream Psychic.*

To unite all race, color, and religion, following her dreams, Ann Marie has written two religiously unaffiliated prayer books, *Spiritual Songs: Letters From My Chest* and *Spiritual Songs II: Blessings From A Sacred Soul*, which people of all faiths can recite.

Ann Marie's writing style is known for making readers feel as though they have made a friend. She has written four books of original inspirational quotations which have also been compiled in one book, *Spiritual Ark: The Enchanted Journey Of Timeless Quotations.*

As a leading voice in the spiritual space, Ann Marie frequently discusses spiritual topics. As a spiritual person, she believes in soul families, reincarnation, and dreams. For this reason, she answers the unanswered questions of life surrounding birth, death, reincarnation, soulmates and twin flames, dreams, miracles, and end of time within her book *Eternal Truth: The Tunnel Of Light*. Readers have referred to this book as one of the must-read and most thought-provoking books.

The Netherlands has been a topic in various books by Ann Marie. As a dream psychic, she constantly has had dreams about this country before ever having any plan to visit the country or any previous knowledge of the contents seen within her dreams. Ann Marie's love and dreams of the Netherlands brought her to write *The Netherlands: Land Of My Dreams* which became an overnight number-one bestseller and topped international bestselling lists.

To capture not just the country but her past inhabitants, Ann Marie wrote for this country, *Everblooming: Through The Twelve Provinces Of The Netherlands*, a keepsake for all generations to come. This book also became an overnight number-one bestseller and topped international bestselling lists. Readers have called this book "the best book ever." They have asked for this book to be included in schools for all to read and cherish.

*Love Letters: The Timeless Treasure* is Ann Marie's thirteenth book. This book also became an overnight bestseller and topped international bestselling lists. Within this book, Ann Marie has gifted her readers fifty of her soul-touching love poems. She calls these poems, love letters. These are individual stories, individual love letters to a beloved, from a lover. In a poetic way, she writes to her twin flame. These poems are her gifts to all loving souls, all twin flames throughout time. All poems have an individual illustration retelling the stories, which Ann Marie designed herself.

*Eternally Beloved: I Shall Never Let You Go* is Ann Marie's fourteenth book. This is her first historical romance fiction, set within the Eighty Years' War-ravaged country, the Netherlands. You can travel through the eyes of Jacobus van Vrederic to the sixteenth century and find out how he battles time to find out love lives on even beyond time. His promise, however, is seen throughout the book and follows him to the sequel as he vows to his eternally beloved, "I shall never let you go."

Now come and step into the sixteenth century once again with Ann Marie as she presents Book Two in the *Kasteel Vrederic* series. Jacobus van Vrederic, a Dutch nobleman, returns to fight a war within a war, through the Dutch Eighty Years' War. Time is his enemy. Through his journey, he tries to rescue some innocent women from being burned at the stakes or becoming a victim at the gallows. Yet Jacobus must through this war fight his own war and find his evermore beloved. Was she too a helpless victim of the witch burnings? Find out how a gallant knight and a daring seer join the returning spirits of Kasteel Vrederic to rescue the evermore beloved of Jacobus van Vrederic, in an eternal, everlasting, emotional, and heartfelt historical romance fiction, *Evermore Beloved: I Shall Never Let You Go.*

## BE MY DESTINY: VOWS FROM THE BEYOND

*Be My Destiny: Vows From The Beyond* is an immortal romance fiction. Through the doors of reincarnation and dreams, travel back to the sixteenth century and revisit twin flames who never united. Yet they have been traveling time to only unite with one another. Always destiny became their enemy. Within this book, you will see how the twenty-first century was a blessed destination for them. As they landed upon this century, the sixteenth-century spirits of Kasteel Vrederic from the *I Shall Never Let You Go* diaries again joined forces to unite once again twin flames. The members of Kasteel Vrederic were waiting for this story to come to life, as this is how it had all begun and so it shall end.

You have her name and know she will always be there for anyone who seeks her. Ann Marie's home is Washington State, USA, yet she travels all around the world to find you, the human with humanity.

For more information about Ann Marie Ruby, any one of her books, or to read her blog posts and articles, subscribe to her website, www.annmarieruby.com.

Follow Ann Marie Ruby on social media:

Twitter: @AnnahMariahRuby
Facebook: @TheAnnMarieRuby
Instagram: @Ann_Marie_Ruby
Pinterest: @TheAnnMarieRuby

# BOOKS BY THE AUTHOR

## *INSPIRATIONAL QUOTATIONS* SERIES:

This series includes four books of original quotations and one omnibus edition.

*Spiritual Travelers:*
*Life's Journey From The Past*
*To The Present*
*For The Future*

*Spiritual*
*Messages:*
*From A Bottle*

*Spiritual Journey:*
*Life's Eternal Blessings*

*Spiritual*
*Inspirations:*
*Sacred Words*
*Of Wisdom*

Omnibus edition contains all four books of original quotations.

*Spiritual Ark:*
*The Enchanted Journey Of Timeless*
*Quotations*

## *SPIRITUAL SONGS* SERIES:

This series includes two original spiritual prayer books.

### *SPIRITUAL SONGS: LETTERS FROM MY CHEST*

When there was no hope, I found hope within these sacred words of prayers, I but call songs. Within this book, I have for you, 100 very sacred prayers.

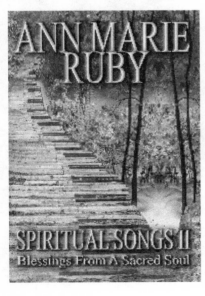

### *SPIRITUAL SONGS II: BLESSINGS FROM A SACRED SOUL*

Prayers are but the sacred doors to an individual's enlightenment. This book has 123 prayers for all humans with humanity.

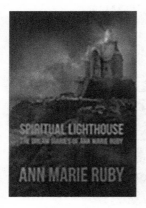

### SPIRITUAL LIGHTHOUSE: THE DREAM DIARIES OF ANN MARIE RUBY

Do you believe in dreams? For within each individual dream, there is a hidden message and a miracle interlinked. Learn the spiritual, scientific, religious, and philosophical aspects of dreams. Walk with me as you travel through forty nights, through the pages of my book.

### THE WORLD HATE CRISIS: THROUGH THE EYES OF A DREAM PSYCHIC

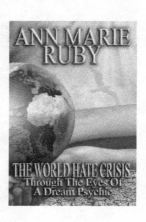

Humans have walked into an age where humanity now is being questioned as hate crimes have reached a catastrophic amount. Let us in union stop this crisis. Pick up my book and see if you too could join me in this fight.

### ETERNAL TRUTH: THE TUNNEL OF LIGHT

Within this book, travel with me through the doors of birth, death, reincarnation, true soulmates and twin flames, dreams, miracles, and the end of time.

### THE NETHERLANDS: LAND OF MY DREAMS

Oh the sacred travelers, be like the mystical river and journey through this blessed land through my book. Be the flying bird of wisdom and learn about a land I call, Heaven on Earth.

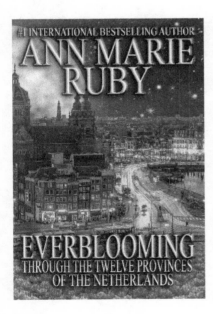

### EVERBLOOMING: THROUGH THE TWELVE PROVINCES OF THE NETHERLANDS

Original poetry and hand-picked tales are bound together in this keepsake book. Come travel with me as I take you through the lives of the Dutch past.

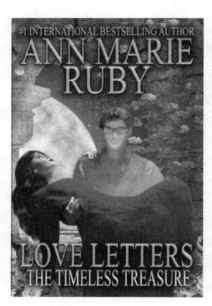

### *LOVE LETTERS: THE TIMELESS TREASURE*

Fifty original timeless treasured love poems are presented with individual illustrations describing each poem.

## *KASTEEL VREDERIC* SERIES:

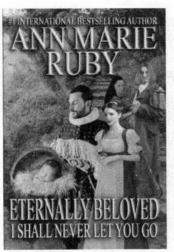

### *ETERNALLY BELOVED: I SHALL NEVER LET YOU GO*

Travel time to the sixteenth century where Jacobus van Vrederic, a beloved lover and father, surmounts time and tide to find the vanished love of his life. On his pursuit, Jacobus discovers secrets that will alter his life evermore. He travels through the Eighty Years' War-ravaged country, the Netherlands as he takes the vow, even if separated by a breath, "Eternally beloved, I shall never let you go."

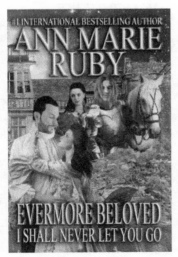

### *EVERMORE BELOVED: I SHALL NEVER LET YOU GO*

Jacobus van Vrederic returns with the devoted spirits of Kasteel Vrederic. A knight and a seer also join him on a quest to find his lost evermore beloved. They journey through a war-ravaged country, the Netherlands, to stop another war which was brewing silently in his land, called the witch hunts. Time was his enemy as he must defeat time and tide to find his evermore beloved wife alive.

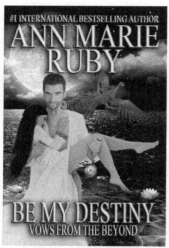

## BE MY DESTINY: VOWS FROM THE BEYOND

Fighting their biggest enemy destiny, twin flames Erasmus van Phillip and Anadhi Newhouse are reborn over and over again only to lose the battle to destiny. Find out if through the helping hands of sacred spirits of the sixteenth century, these eternal twin flames are finally able to unite in the twenty-first century, as they say, "Reincarnation is a blessing if only you are mine."

*Coming Soon*

**HEART BEATS YOUR NAME: VOWS FROM THE BEYOND**

## HEART BEATS YOUR NAME: VOWS FROM THE BEYOND

The fourth book in this series is coming soon.

*Coming Soon*

**ENTRANCED
BELOVED:
I SHALL NEVER
LET YOU GO**

## ENTRANCED BELOVED: I SHALL NEVER LET YOU GO

The fifth book in this series is coming soon.

CPSIA information can be obtained
at www.ICGtesting.com
Printed in the USA
LVHW112224191122
733619LV00022B/179